HOME ALONe 2

LOST IN NEW YORK

HOME ALONe 2
LOST IN NEW YORK

A novelization by A.L. Singer
Based on the screenplay by John Hughes

Hippo Books
Scholastic Children's Books
London

TWENTIETH CENTURY FOX PRESENTS A JOHN HUGHES PRODUCTION A CHRIS COLUMBUS FILM
MACAULAY CULKIN JOE PESCI DANIEL STERN HOME ALONE 2
FILM EDITOR RAJA GOSNELL PRODUCTION DESIGNER SANDY VENEZIANO DIRECTOR OF PHOTOGRAPHY JULIO MACAT EXECUTIVE PRODUCER MARK RADCLIFFE
WRITTEN AND PRODUCED BY JOHN HUGHES DIRECTED BY CHRIS COLUMBUS COLOR BY DELUXE®

1991 TWENTIETH CENTURY FOX

Scholastic Children's Books,
Scholastic Publications Ltd,
7-9 Pratt Street, London NW1 0AE, UK

Scholastic Inc.,
730 Broadway, New York, NY 10003, USA

Scholastic Canada Ltd,
123 Newkirk Road, Richmond Hill,
Ontario, Canada L4C 3G5

Ashton Scholastic Pty Ltd,
PO Box 579, Gosford, New South Wales,
Australia

Ashton Scholastic Ltd,
Private Bag 1, Penrose, Auckland,
New Zealand

First published in the US by Scholastic Inc., 1992
First published in the UK by Scholastic Publications Ltd, 1992

ISBN 0 590 55161 2

Printed by Cox & Wyman Ltd, Reading, Berks

10 9 8 7 6 5 4 3 2 1

Prologue

Kevin McCallister.

That was the kid's name. There he was, smirking out the living room window. And waving! He was actually waving!

Harry Lyme felt his blood boil. He squirmed in the backseat of the police car, pulling at his handcuffs. His partner, Marv Murchens, just stared dumbly out the window. As the car backed out of the McCallister driveway, both men lurched forward in their seat.

"We got 'em, Chief . . ." the policeman said into his radio. "Yep . . . the Wet Bandits . . . and you won't believe this, but it was a little kid who caught 'em!"

The two cops burst out laughing in the front seat. Marv laughed along with them.

"Knock it off!" Harry said to his partner through gritted teeth.

Done in by a kid. Harry couldn't get over it. He and Marv had planned the perfect crime. They had cased the Mc-Callister house. They knew the family was leaving on Christmas vacation. They knew how to beat the security system. And they'd had plenty of experience robbing other houses.

How were they to know the McCallister kid would be left home by mistake? And how were they to know that little punk could boobytrap the whole house — and keep them there long enough to call the cops?

If it wasn't for Marv, they might have pulled it off. At least that was how Harry saw it. Marv was too easily fooled by the kid's tricks. Sometimes Marv's head was in the clouds. "The Wet Bandits" — that name was Marv's idea. "Every famous team of crooks has to have a nickname," Marv had said. So every time they robbed a house, he left a faucet running. It was supposed to be like a calling card. Was that ridiculous or what?

Well, it didn't matter, Harry thought. Soon he and Marv were going to be free. With a grunt, Harry managed to reach into his back pocket. He clasped his fingers around a tiny, homemade lock pick. As he pulled it out, Marv gave him a knowing smile.

He twisted his right hand around, inserted the pick. He poked, turned . . .

Snap!

Harry smiled. His hand was loose. The cops were chatting in the front seat and they hadn't heard a thing. And the car was about to stop at a train crossing.

Quickly, quietly, he unlocked his other hand. This escape was going to be a cinch. He and Marv were about to be free men. And their first stop would be the McCallister house.

Kevin McCallister shuffled into the dark living room. He yawned and looked toward the front door. There were his toys, all lined up for attack. And there was the electric barbecue starter, wrapped around the metal doorknob. The starter was cool now, but a few hours ago it was red hot. And when that crooked goon, Harry, touched the doorknob on the other side — boy, did he get a shock.

Well, it was all over now, except for the cleanup.

With a sigh, Kevin scooped up the toys. Out of the corner of his eye, he noticed the security chain was hanging loose. He reached toward it with his free hand.

"Better safe than sorry . . ." he murmured to himself.

WHAAMM!

The door swung open with the force of a tornado. It crashed to the floor, its hinges ripping off the doorjamb.

And there, standing in the jagged door frame, were the two people Kevin hoped never to see again.

"Merry Christmas, little fella," said Harry with a sickening smile.

"Ho, ho, ho," said Marv.

"Aaaaaaagh!" Screaming, Kevin spun around and ran to the back of the house.

Harry and Marv clomped along behind him. "It's all over for you, pal!" Harry called out.

"You're all out of tricks!" Marv added.

But they were wrong. Dead wrong. Kevin didn't know what he was going to do — but he would do something!

He barreled out the back door. The night air was a sudden shock to his skin. His feet slipped in the snow as he scrambled through the backyard and into the side door of the garage.

Wheeling around, Kevin slammed the door shut and locked it — just as Marv banged into the door. For a brief moment, Kevin caught a glimpse of the bandit. Marv's tall, thin frame was hunched over the doorknob. As he rattled it, he gritted his teeth angrily.

Kevin ran straight for a ladder in the back. He'd have some time before Marv broke in. Marv was a dork, he decided. On any other person, long sideburns and a goatee might look sinister and devilish. On Marv, they looked goofy.

Harry was no genius either. He was short, balding, stubby, and mean. Harry considered himself the brains of the outfit. Maybe, just maybe, that was true.

But that wasn't saying much.

Oh, well, Kevin thought, if I could beat them once, I can beat them again. He scrambled up the ladder. It led up to a small section of flooring, supported by the garage's rafters. Two sides of the floor connected with the garage wall. From the other two sides, you could look out over the garage, like a balcony.

Crashhh! came the sound of breaking glass.

Kevin peeked over the edge of the floor. Marv's hand was reaching through the broken window of the side door, groping for the knob. Out of the corner of his eye, Kevin spotted Harry's fingers reaching through a hole in the *front* door of the garage.

Time for some drastic action. Kevin crawled to the garage-door opener, which hung just below one of the rafters. He flicked the switch, and the front door began to roll upward.

With Harry on it.

"Whooooaaa . . ." Harry cried, his fingers caught in the hole.

The door lifted him straight up and into the garage. When it stopped, Kevin could see Harry lying flat on top of it. Fortunately, the flooring was out of Harry's reach.

The opening door had automatically turned on the garage light. Kevin looked around. There was all kinds of junk up there — an old lawn mower, some sections of a metal rain gutter, a set of dumbbells, a baseball pitching machine, lots of rope, some lawn furniture, and a dime-store mannequin.

Perfect.

Quickly he dragged the mannequin to the edge of the floor, so that its feet dangled over. He tied one end of a long rope to the mannequin's neck and the other end to the starter of the lawn mower. Below, he could hear Marv rummaging around in the garage. Wasting no time, Kevin tied another rope from the lawn mower to the release lever of the pitching machine.

Then he pulled up an old lawn chair and sat down to watch the show.

Marv's footsteps stopped. Kevin could see a hand closing around the mannequin's foot. "I got him!" Marv cried out.

Marv yanked hard. With a jerk, the mannequin disappeared over the edge of the flooring. The rope pulled tight, drawing the starter cord right out of the lawn mower.

Whiiiirrrr . . . pock! Pock! Chucka-chucka . . . With a sputter and a wheeze, the mower roared to life. It began moving toward the edge of the floor — right above Marv's head.

From his perch on the garage door, Harry looked up. Kevin smiled and waved at him.

"Marv!" Harry shouted. "Heads up!"

In a puff of blue smoke, the lawn mower fell off the flooring. Kevin shielded his eyes.

There was a thud. Marv's scream echoed through the garage.

The rope to the pitching machine snapped taut. It pulled on the handle, and a hardball shot out — directly at Harry!

"Yeeoow!" Harry cried.

Kevin looked out over the garage. A cloud of exhaust fumes rose up from the floor. It circled around the garage door, where Harry was rubbing a huge bump on his forehead. When the smoke cleared below, there was Marv. His face was covered with nicks and cuts — and the top of his hair was shaved flat!

Crreeeeak! The garage door began sagging under Harry's weight. Suddenly, with two loud bangs, the hinges snapped out of the wall.

The door slammed shut. It tossed Harry backward. Flailing his arms, he landed in a heap on the McCallister driveway.

Kevin scrambled to the pile of junk and picked up a long section of the rain gutter. Would it be long enough to reach the open window in the front of the garage? The open window *just above where Harry was*? At the edge of the flooring, he reached out with it . . . and reached . . .

Yes!

The end of the gutter rested on the window ledge. Kevin balanced a ten-pound dumbbell on top of the gutter and let it roll downward, right toward the window.

Outside the garage, Harry picked himself up. He rubbed his head. His bump was the size of a billiard ball. His back felt broken. And what was that rumbling noise?

He looked up toward the noise. He saw the gutter pipe sticking through the window. The rumbling got louder. Something was coming down the pipe.

When he saw the dumbbell, he froze. His brain told him to move, but his body wouldn't obey.

All he could do was open his mouth and scream.

HOME ALONe 2

LOST IN NEW YORK

Chapter 1

"Aaaaaaggh!"

Harry bolted upright. His bedsheet was soaked with sweat. The hallway light shone weakly through his prison bars, casting black stripes across the cell.

He blinked once, twice. *I was dreaming,* he said to himself.

The reality came flooding back: He and Marv hadn't escaped the police car. They'd gone to jail.

It had been a whole year since that night at the McCallisters'. A whole year since the kid had foiled their robbery. A whole year of terrible food, stinking jail cells, and bad dreams.

He stood up and clutched his cell bars with frustration.

Down the hall, in another cell, Marv awoke with a start. His eyes were wide with terror. Shaking, he walked over to his sleeping cellmate's bed. "I — I just had a bad dream," Marv said. "Would you mind if I crawled in with you?"

Without a word, Marv's cellmate sat up, his eyes bloodshot and his teeth clenched with rage. The bed creaked under his two hundred pounds. With a growl, he picked Marv up and hurled him against the wall.

Harry winced at the sound of Marv thudding against the wall. That rotten kid was still giving *both* of them nightmares!

Peering angrily into the dusty dimness of the prison hallway, Harry muttered, "If I ever see that kid again, he's history!"

Fat chance he *would* ever see that kid again, though. If he and Marv ever escaped, they'd skip the country. They'd leave Chicago far behind.

But still, you never knew . . .

Chapter 2

It was a typical three days before Christmas at the McCallister house. Lots of food, a couple of presents already under the tree, everybody feeling pressure, a fire in the fireplace . . . and one other crucial ingredient.

Chaos.

McCallisters young and old screamed, yelled, joked, whined, yawned, burped, complained, laughed, and ran up and down stairs. In the McCallister house, *every* creature was stirring — every creature, that is, except for Kevin.

Upstairs, Kevin was taking a break. He stretched himself out on his parents' bed and tuned out. Tuned out the noise from the house, tuned out the sound of his parents' bedroom TV set. He was used to noise by now. At ten years old, he was the youngest in the house, so it had been like this his whole life.

That night was worse than most, though. In a little while, they were all going to the big Christmas Pageant at school. The next morning, they were all going to leave for the annual McCallister Christmas trip. This year they were going to Miami, Florida — sunny, warm . . .

Boring.

Kevin sighed. Who wanted to go to *Florida* for Christmas? There was no snow there. What did they do, string Christmas lights on palm trees?

That was the worst part. As far as Kevin was concerned, it wasn't Christmas without a real, live Christmas tree. With lots of lights and ornaments and tinsel. Preferably one that stunk up the house with pine. It was the one thing that made him feel tingly and warm during this season — well, that and hot chocolate. Otherwise, Christmas mostly meant yelling and fighting and asking dumb questions . . .

One thing was for sure, though. On a crazy night like this, you didn't complain. It was best to just get out of the way. Kevin was already packed for the trip and dressed for the concert. While everyone else was going nuts, he had plenty of time to test his new Talkboy. There was no *end* to what you could do with it. For instance, you could record family members saying stupid things, then play it back later to embarrass them. That was always good for a chuckle.

And there were plenty of family members to record, saying plenty of stupid things. Kevin had two brothers (Buzz and Jeff) and two sisters (Megan and Linnie). But that wasn't all. His uncle Frank and aunt Leslie were visiting with their kids: Fuller, Brooke, Tracey, and Sondra. His cousin Rod, who lived with Uncle Frank and Aunt Leslie, was there, too.

Add Kevin's parents, Peter and Kate McCallister, and you got fourteen McCallisters. In one house. No wonder it was so loud.

"Has anybody seen my sun block?" his cousin Tracey screeched as she barreled down the stairs.

"What's the point of going to Florida if you're going to put on sun block?" answered Sondra as she barreled up the stairs.

"I don't care if I age like an old suitcase. I'm getting toasted!" That was Megan. She was going downstairs.

"So you'll be a skag with a slightly darker shade of tan." Typical wit and wisdom from Buzz (going up).

"He's jealous because he doesn't get tan! His freckles just connect!" Linnie speaking.

Kevin's mom bustled into the bedroom and put some of her clothes into an open suitcase. "Honey, are you packed?" she asked, walking into the bathroom.

"Yes," Kevin said softly into his Talkboy. He quickly rewound and played back on high volume.

"Yes!" the Talkboy replied.

"All the stuff I put out for you?" she called.

Kevin rewound and played again: *"Yes!"*

Mrs. McCallister came out of the bathroom, holding a small bag full of toiletries. "Did you see what Grandma Penelope sent you for the trip?"

"Let me guess." Kevin tried to think of the most babyish toy possible. Grandma Penelope seemed to think he was still three. "Donald Duck slippers?"

Kevin's mom pulled a small plastic container out of the suitcase. BONGO THE CLOWN! its label said. "It's an inflatable clown to play with in the pool."

Kevin rolled his eyes in disgust. He caught a glimpse of the TV set at the foot of the bed. A game show host was gabbing away: "Thanks for joining us on the new Celebrity Ding-Dang-Dong! Good night!"

Then an image of a big hotel came on, with flags flying over the doors, limos parked in front, and towers rising from the roof. An announcer's voice said, "Guests of the new Celebrity Ding-Dang-Dong stay at the world-renowned Plaza Hotel, New York's most exciting hotel experience. For reservations call toll-free, 1-800-759-3000 . . ."

Ding-a-ling-a-ling!

Kevin recognized that sound. It was a

small bell the McCallisters took out for Christmas every year. For as long as Kevin could remember, his mom would use it to wake up the family on Christmas morning and to summon them for dinner. It went with them whenever they took a Christmas trip. "Can't forget this!" his mom said, putting it in the suitcase.

Kevin smiled. The bell was another thing he liked about Christmas.

"Honey?" Mr. McCallister said, rushing into the room. "Where's the camcorder battery?"

"It's in the charger, by the nightstand," Mrs. McCallister replied. "And don't just pack the battery this time. Take the charger, too. We'll need it."

Mr. McCallister reached underneath the nightstand. The charger was plugged into a three-outlet attachment, which he pulled out of the wall.

He didn't realize what was attached to the *other* two plugs: the digital alarm clock and the digital clock radio. Silently, they both went blank.

As Mr. McCallister pulled the charger's plug out of the attachment, he looked at

Kevin. "You better get your tie on, son," he said.

"My tie's in my room and I can't go in there," Kevin replied. "Uncle Frank is taking a shower in the kids' bathroom. He doesn't want me to walk in and see him."

"Your bedroom is *attached* to the bathroom, it's not *in* the bathroom," Mr. McCallister said, plugging the three-outlet attachment back into the wall. "Just run in and get your tie. Uncle Frank won't even know."

"All right," Kevin said. Clutching his Talkboy, he got off the bed and headed into the upstairs hallway.

Mr. McCallister rushed around to finish packing. Mrs. McCallister freshened her makeup in the mirror.

Everyone was in a mad rush. Too rushed to notice the small, dull-gray readouts on the clock and the radio, flashing over and over:

12:00 . . .
12:00 . . .
12:00 . . .

9

Chapter 3

Kevin almost ran right into Megan and Sondra, who were dragging huge suitcases out of their bedroom. Megan gave him her very favorite facial expression — a sneer. "Dad says we have to have all our suitcases down by the door before we go to the Christmas Pageant," she said.

"Are you my new mother?" Kevin retorted.

"Remember what happened last year?" Sondra said.

Kevin held the Talkboy out and pressed PLAY. *"Brrrup!"* came the noise of a loud belch.

"You're nauseating," said Megan.

Kevin laughed and ran into his bedroom. On the far wall, the bathroom door was slightly open. Wisps of steam billowed out. The shower was running, and Uncle Frank was singing "Cool Jerk" at the top of his lungs.

Singing? That wasn't the word. *Bellowing* was more like it — or *honking*. Uncle Frank's voice was subhuman. It was the only sound in the world that made Kevin lose his appetite. To be honest, Uncle Frank was not on Kevin's list of top ten favorite people. He was always yelling at Kevin for no reason.

It might be fun to capture Uncle Frank's singing on tape. With a tiny smile, Kevin pressed RECORD on his Talkboy and crept closer to the open door.

Uncle Frank kept squawking for a few moments, then stopped. He peered out from behind the shower curtain. "Hey, get out of here, you nosy little creep — or I'll come out and slap you silly!"

Whoops.

Kevin shut off the Talkboy, grabbed the tie off his bed, and ran out.

By the time Kevin finished tying his tie, the rest of the family was beginning to climb into the two McCallister station wagons. He pulled on his coat and ran outside.

Yelling, fussing, arguing, they arrived at the school — just in time. Kevin began feeling nervous. All of his brothers and sisters were in the choir, but he was the only one with a solo. He checked his collar, his hair, his shirt buttons, his zipper. There was nothing worse than being laughed at in public for something dumb, like an open fly.

Once they arrived at the school, Kevin felt fine. And when he lined up backstage with the rest of the choir, he was actually excited.

Each choir member took an electric, battery-operated candle. One by one, they walked onto a set of risers, the shorter kids in the front and the taller in the back.

In the audience, Mr. and Mrs. McCallister beamed with pride. So did Aunt Leslie. Uncle Frank was fast asleep.

Kevin's stomach began fluttering. The auditorium was packed. He could see his mom and dad smiling at him. Christmas decorations were hanging all over the place, but at that moment it was hard to get into the spirit. He looked at the music teacher, who gave him a big smile.

Behind him, Buzz was smiling, too, but for a different reason. He was cooking up a plan — a plan that had very little to do with the spirit of Christmas.

The teacher tapped the music stand with a baton. As the house lights dimmed, the audience fell silent. On a cue from the teacher, the choir began to sing a Christmas tune.

Kevin's solo was coming up in the middle of the song. He swallowed and cleared his throat.

"Kevin's solo is coming up," Mrs. McCallister whispered to her husband. "Tell Leslie."

"Kevin's solo is coming up," Mr. McCallister whispered to Aunt Leslie.

Aunt Leslie turned to Uncle Frank and elbowed him in the ribs. "Guurrgglh," he muttered.

Buzz grabbed the candle from the kid next to him. Slowly, Buzz began moving both candles to a spot right behind Kevin's ears.

With a deep breath, Kevin began to sing his solo: "Christmas time means laughter, toboggans in the snow . . ."

The light from Buzz's candles shone through Kevin's ears, making them glow. A few people in the audience began to giggle.

Kevin ignored them. Probably someone burped or something, he figured. "Caroling together," he sang, "with faces all aglow!"

At those words, the audience exploded with laughter. Kevin was completely baffled. What was going on here? "Stockings on the mantle, a wreath on the door . . ." He kept singing, but now even the choir was laughing!

That was when he felt the warmth behind his ears. Slowly he turned around. "And my merriest Christmas needs just one thing more . . ."

There was Buzz. The King of Geeks. The Meister of Dorkmeisters. One small step up from a bilge rat, one giant step below a warthog. And he was holding those candles, grinning at the audience as if he were a movie star!

14

Kevin reared back and socked him in the stomach.

"Oof!" Buzz gasped. As he fell backward, he grabbed the boys on either side of him.

One boy tumbled off with Buzz. The other grabbed a fourth boy, who lost his balance. He knocked down a girl, who toppled into another girl. She stumbled into two boys, who fell off the side of the risers. One by one, the choir members fell like dominoes.

The music teacher stared in shock. Decorations flew, wreaths fell from the walls, and candlelights arched through the air like fireflies.

Finally, when the last choir member hit the floor, the Christmas tree collapsed in a tangle of broken lights and ornaments.

As the curtain fell on the pandemonium, Kevin tried as hard as he could to pummel the living daylights out of his older brother.

Still, from the audience he could hear the familiar panicked shriek of his mom's voice:

"Kevin!"

Later that night, Buzz and Kevin sat in two chairs by the McCallister living-room fireplace. Around them stood the other twelve members of the family. Their arms were folded, their eyes glaring.

Buzz stood up and cleared his throat. "I want to apologize to you all for whatever displeasure I caused you. And I want to apologize to my brother. Kevin, I'm sorry. My prank was immature and ill-timed."

"Immature or not," Uncle Frank said, "it was pretty darn hilarious!"

Kevin's dad shot him an angry look. Uncle Frank shrugged and looked at the floor.

"I can assure you all," Buzz continued, "there will be absolutely no more she-nanigans from me. Christmas is a sacred, happy, loving, caring time of the year, and everybody in the family of man should go along with that." He paused, furrowed his brow, and added, "Amen."

Mrs. McCallister smiled proudly. "That was very nice, Buzz! Now, Kevin, what do you have to say?"

Kevin looked at her in shock. She *be-*

lieved that sneaky, two-faced, trouble-making liar?

Buzz pretended to scratch his nose. Under his cupped hand, he wiggled his retainer at Kevin and muttered, "Beat that, you little trout sniffer."

Kevin felt like exploding with anger. He glanced around the room. They were all looking at him. They all expected *him* to apologize to Buzz! How unfair was that?

"I'm not sorry," Kevin said. "I did what I did because Buzz humiliated me. And since he gets away with everything, I let him have it. And since you're all so stupid to believe his lies, I don't care if your idiotic Florida trip gets wrecked or not. Who wants to spend Christmas in a tropical climate anyway?"

He turned on his heels and stomped away.

"Kevin!" his mom shouted angrily.

"If you walk out of here," his dad said, "you'll sleep on the third floor!"

Typical. Whenever they wanted to punish him — which was at least once a day — they sent him to the attic room.

When he was a kid, it used to scare him, but not anymore. "So what else is new?" he said.

"You better not wreck my trip, you little sourpuss," Uncle Frank said. "Your dad's paying good money for it."

Kevin ran up both flights of stairs and plopped down on the attic room bed. "They're all a bunch of jerks," he murmured.

Just as he expected, he heard his mom's footsteps coming up the stairs. She pushed open the door and came in. Her face was all tight and serious, the way it got when she needed to yell at him.

"Last time we all tried to go on a trip," she said, "we had a problem that started just like this."

"Yeah," Kevin retorted. "With me getting dumped on."

"That isn't what happened last time, and it isn't what's happening this time. Buzz apologized to you."

"Then he wiggled his retainer at me! He didn't mean what he said. He's just sucking up to you!"

"Your father's spending a lot of money

to take us all to Florida."

Kevin turned away. "That's his problem."

"You sit up here for a while and think things over. When you're ready to apologize to Buzz and the rest of the family —"

"I'm not apologizing to Buzz!" Kevin shot back. "I'd rather kiss a toilet seat."

"Then you can stay up here the rest of the night."

"Fine! I don't want to be down there anyway. I can't trust anybody in this family. And you know what? If I had my own money, I'd go on my own vacation — by myself. Alone, without any of you guys! And I'd have the most fun of my life!"

His mom glared at him. "You got your wish last year. Maybe you'll get it again this year!"

She was right. He *had* wished to be left home alone last year. With a shrug, he said, "I hope so."

Mrs. McCallister shook her head and sighed. Then she wearily turned and walked downstairs.

Kevin watched her go. Maybe she was

right. Maybe if he wished hard enough, he would get a vacation all by himself. To a place where no one would bother him, no one would make fun of him, and no one would cause him any trouble.

What a thought.

With a smile on his face, Kevin felt himself fall helplessly, deeply asleep.

One by one, for the next hour or so, the rest of the family trudged up the stairs. The night had worn everyone out, and tomorrow promised to be a big day. Not one of them had trouble falling right to sleep.

And not one of them bothered to check the two clocks in the master bedroom.

As the lights went out, the McCallister house was swallowed in the dark winter night. A frigid wind screamed in from the north, but no one heard it. It bent trees, it whipped branches against the house, it stirred up trash cans and blew rubbish into the street.

For a moment, a crumpled page of that day's newspaper smacked against the front door. It flipped open to a two-column headline:

"WET BANDITS" ESCAPE DURING
PRISON RIOT!

Then, as fast as it came, it flew away
into the night.

Chapter 4

Knock-knock-knock!

The driver of the airport van pounded
on the McCallister door, but no one answered. He looked at his watch. It was
eight o'clock in the morning, and the family should have been ready by now. The
flight was at nine, and O'Hare Airport
was a long drive. He turned to the other
driver, who was waiting by the second
van. Both men shrugged.

"Maybe they left already," said the
driver at the door.

"Try the bell again," replied the other
man.

RIIINNNNGGG!

Upstairs the McCallister family slept. From each room came the soft rhythms of breathing. In the master bedroom, the clock radio and alarm clock blinked silently.

RIIINNNNGGG!

Mr. and Mrs. McCallister sat bolt upright in their bed. Their eyes went straight to the clock.

12:00 . . .

12:00 . . .

12:00 . . .

They leapt out of bed, their faces frozen in disbelief. *"We did it again!"* they shrieked at the same time.

Their words rang through the house like a battle cry. In an instant the second floor flew into action. It was every McCallister for him or herself. Fourteen pairs of feet hit the floor. Fourteen dresser drawers were pulled open. Fourteen sets of clothes were thrown on. And fourteen people managed to grab fourteen toothbrushes from three bathrooms.

In a flurry of crashing doors, thundering footsteps, and screaming voices, all

McCallisters managed to dress, go to the bathroom, grab suitcases, and rush downstairs.

In exactly three and a half minutes.

The two drivers watched in awe as the family burst out the front door.

"Our McCallisters in the front van!" Kevin's mom announced. "The other McCallisters in the second van!"

Uncle Frank pulled on his parka as he shuffled past Mrs. McCallister. "I know I shouldn't complain about a free trip," he said, "but you people give the worst darn wakeup calls!"

Mrs. McCallister ignored the comment. "Frank, do you have the tickets?" she asked.

"Leslie's in charge of the tickets," Uncle Frank said. "I'm in charge of the hotel reservations."

Aunt Leslie was the second to last out of the house. "Got 'em, Kate!" she shouted to Mrs. McCallister.

Last was Mr. McCallister. "Why is it," he moaned, "that every time we go on a trip, we leave in a state of confusion?"

"Lock up!" his wife replied.

Mr. McCallister quickly locked the

front door and ran to the back of the first van. As he threw his luggage in, his wife called out to the second van, "How many do you have, Les?"

"Seven," Aunt Leslie answered.

"I have seven, too," Mrs. McCallister said.

"Fourteen," she and Aunt Leslie chimed together.

The adults climbed into the vans — Mr. and Mrs. McCallister in the first, Aunt Leslie and Uncle Frank in the second. Just to be sure, Mrs. McCallister counted everyone in her van *again*: her husband, Buzz, Megan, Linnie, Jeff — and, yes, Kevin.

Kevin was definitely there. She could see his face clearly. There was no way she would make the same mistake she made last year, no matter how much of a rush they were in.

"Let's go," Mrs. McCallister said to the driver. "We're all here."

Kevin sat glumly in the front bucket seat, clutching his plane ticket. In a way, he was glad they hadn't forgotten him. At least it showed they cared. But what did he have to show for that? Two weeks with a jerky brother and a family that didn't understand him. In Florida.

Some fun.

"This time I'll carry my own ticket," Kevin said. "Just in case you guys try and ditch me."

The vans roared away. They sped through quiet streets and onto the highway, which was just starting to clog with traffic.

Weaving from lane to lane, the vans made it to O'Hare Airport. They screeched to a stop at the entrance. A clock above them read eight fifty-five.

"We're on the nine o'clock flight to Miami!" Mr. McCallister shouted at a team of skycaps.

The skycaps grabbed carts and rushed to the vans. As they loaded luggage, Uncle Frank frantically handed out tickets.

"Who am I sitting next to?" Megan insisted.

"You can work that out on the plane!" Mrs. McCallister snapped.

"I have to go to the bathroom!" Fuller shouted.

"We didn't have breakfast!" Linnie complained.

Kevin wanted desperately to drown out the noise. He pulled his Talkboy out of his coat pocket and plugged in the earphones. He pressed PLAY, but no sound came out.

"Dad?" he said. "I need batteries."

Mr. McCallister was busily herding kids through the airport door. His travel bag was slung over his shoulder, and Kevin was sure there were batteries in it.

"I don't have any batteries," Mr. McCallister called over his shoulder.

Kevin sneaked up behind him and reached into the bag.

"Not right now, Kevin," his dad said.

"Everybody inside," Mrs. McCallister yelled. "Let's go!"

"Wait a minute," Kevin protested. "I need batteries!"

To their right, one of the skycaps was handing Uncle Frank some luggage tags. Uncle Frank took the tags and leaned close to Kevin's dad. "Uh, Peter?" he said softly. "I want to tip these guys, but the smallest I have is a twenty. Can you take care of them? I'll pay you back."

Typical Uncle Frank, Kevin thought.

Mr. McCallister put his shoulder bag

down on the ground. He unzipped it, took out his wallet, and pulled a ten-dollar bill from it.

Kevin saw his golden moment of opportunity. As soon as his dad put his wallet back, Kevin swiped the bag. "I'll carry it for you!" he said.

Mr. McCallister was too preoccupied to notice. "What gate do we go to?" he shouted to the skycap.

"E fifteen!" the skycap replied.

"That's all the way at the end?" Mr. McCallister asked.

The skycap nodded. "Last gate. You better run!"

The race was on. Kevin and his family sprinted through the airport concourse like a herd of wild horses. Their footsteps clattered loudly. People leapt aside to avoid the onslaught.

And Kevin trotted along happily in the midst of it all, rummaging through his dad's shoulder bag for batteries. He found an instant camera, a wallet, an address book, some magazines, an envelope filled with cash . . . and a spanking new pack of AA batteries!

Victory!

As he loaded the batteries into the Talkboy, he slowed down. Jeff passed him by, then Linnie. Finally Mr. McCallister went huffing and puffing by, his tan-colored overcoat flapping out on both sides.

Kevin picked up his pace. But it was hard to figure out which way the batteries went. Where was the plus sign?

He squinted down into the battery compartment. There it was! Quickly he shot a glance upward. The tan overcoat was still in front of him.

He loaded in the batteries, then looked up again. The overcoat swerved left.

Kevin followed behind, looking back down at the Talkboy for the last time. He closed up the compartment, turned the Talkboy on, and hooked it onto his belt.

But he had lost ground. The overcoat was disappearing into the crowd ahead of him. "Dad, wait up!" Kevin called out.

He elbowed his way through the throng of people. Up ahead, he caught sight of his dad's overcoat, moving past the ticket agent and up the corridor to the plane.

"Last call for American Airlines Flight one-nine-one . . ." began a muffled announcement over the loudspeakers. Kevin could barely hear it, but he flew into a panic.

The ticket agent bundled up the boarding passes she had collected. As she began closing the corridor door, Kevin screamed, "Wait!"

Waving his boarding pass, he sprinted toward her. He held out his free hand to stop the door from closing.

Wham! He barreled into the ticket agent full-force. Her boarding passes flew into the air — along with Kevin's.

Dazed, the agent watched the passes rain down around her head.

"I'm sorry," Kevin said, out of breath.

The agent forced a smile. "That's all right. Are you on this flight?"

"Yeah. So's my family, but they're already on the plane and I don't want to get left behind!"

"Do you have a boarding pass?"

"It's — " Kevin looked forlornly at the mess on the floor.

"We have to close up here," called an airline official from the check-in counter. "They've got to go!"

"He dropped his boarding pass," the agent said.

"They can't leave!" Kevin pleaded. "This happened to me last year and it almost wrecked my Christmas!"

The official began walking over to him. "You're sure your family's on this flight?"

"My dad got on just before I crashed into this lady," Kevin explained.

The official nodded solemnly, then turned to the ticket agent. "Let him board, but make sure he locates his family before you leave him."

"Okay," the agent replied. Stepping through the door, she said to Kevin, "Come on!"

Kevin raced behind her down the corridor and into the plane. Around them, flight attendants and passengers bustled and jostled into each other.

"Do you see your family?" the agent asked.

Kevin looked into the first-class section. That was where his mom and dad always sat. (The kids, of course, sat in coach.)

Sure enough, there was the familiar

overcoat. Kevin breathed easier. His dad was facing away from him, loading something into an overhead compartment. Even though Kevin couldn't actually see his dad's face, he could recognize that overcoat anywhere.

"That's my dad," Kevin said.

The agent smiled. "Okay. Have a Merry Christmas."

As she walked out of the plane, Kevin took the nearest empty seat. He stuffed his dad's travel bag under the seat in front, took out his Talkboy, then sat down.

It felt great to be finally settled in. The engines were humming, and the plane was beginning to move. Next stop would be Miami!

That didn't sound so bad, after all. A little sunshine, a little swimming . . .

As Kevin looked around the plane, he had a funny feeling. Not one of his siblings was anywhere to be seen.

Probably all in the bathroom, he thought. Besides, it was a huge plane and there was no way he could see all the seats.

He turned back around and put on his headphones. And just in time, because the pilot's dull speech was beginning:

"Ladies and gentleman, on behalf of the staff and flight crew, I'd like to welcome you aboard American Airlines Flight one-nine-one to — "

Kevin pressed PLAY and sat back. An earsplitting rock tune drowned out the rest of the announcement:

" — New York! Our flying time will be an hour and fifty minutes. Sit back and enjoy the flight."

Kevin didn't hear a word of it. He closed his eyes and listened to his tape. Had he kept his eyes open a moment longer, he might have seen the man with the overcoat turn around. He might have caught a good look at his face — a face that didn't resemble his dad's in the least.

But by the time Kevin opened his eyes, the man was hidden by the back of his first-class seat.

Across the airport, on another runway, a 727 prepared to take off. Its destination was Miami, Florida.

Mr. McCallister sighed with relief as he sank into his seat. "I didn't think we'd make it," he said.

He looked at his wife, who gave him a tense smile.

"Is something wrong?" Mr. McCallister asked.

"It's that feeling again."

"You forgot something?"

Mrs. McCallister shrugged. "I know I didn't, but I just have that *feeling*."

"Bad memories, that's all," her husband said. "We did everything, we brought everything. We're all here. There's nothing to worry about." He smiled warmly and put his arm around her shoulder.

As the airplane lifted off the ground, thirteen McCallisters headed for sunny Miami, Florida.

Chapter 5

Kevin was the first one off the airplane. He ran down the enclosed corridor to the airport, toting his dad's shoulder bag.

He hadn't seen any of them during the flight. It seemed a little strange, but he hadn't minded a bit. His Talkboy was great company.

Just inside the waiting-area entrance, Kevin turned around to wait for his family. He watched the passengers as they trudged out of the plane.

He shifted his weight impatiently. This was getting boring. Where *were* they? Still in the bathroom? Impossible.

When the flight attendants started

leaving, Kevin had a sinking feeling. He'd lost them. All thirteen of them somehow managed to sneak by without him seeing them.

Kevin tried to keep his cool. They had to be around somewhere. He searched through the waiting area, then walked out into the hallway. Left and right, people with down coats jostled against him. He kept his eyes moving, checking out candy stores, fast-food joints, pastry carts.

No McCallister in sight.

Finally he wandered into the men's room. He could see feet under two of the stall doors. He knocked on one. "Dad?"

"Get lost," a gruff voice barked back.

He knocked on the other. "Uncle Frank?"

"Get out of here!" That sounded like something Uncle Frank would say — but it wasn't Uncle Frank's voice.

He left the men's room. Just to his right there was a balcony that overlooked the main concourse. He walked over and looked at the crowd below.

His eyes darted from face to face. People swarmed around each other like bees in winter clothing, no one standing still long enough to —

Winter clothing?

Wait a minute. What was going on? Where were the shorts and sandals? This was Florida!

Kevin sped downstairs to the terminal. He went straight to a long, high desk and stood on tiptoe. Behind the desk, a woman in an airline uniform was talking on the phone. "Excuse me," Kevin said. "How come it's so cold outside? Isn't it supposed to be in the seventies? And also, I don't see any palm trees or senior citizens in shorts."

The woman put her hand over the receiver. "I'll be with you in a minute."

"Okay." Kevin stepped down and waited. He glanced around the terminal, watching the people race about. Through the plate glass doors he could see buses and taxis loading passengers, and a hazy city skyline in the distance.

Huh?

Kevin's eyes widened. This was some skyline. It made Chicago's look puny. Miami *couldn't* be so big.

He stepped back up to the counter. "Uh, I know you told me to wait, but this is an emergency," he insisted.

"Hold, please," the woman said into the phone. She turned politely to Kevin. "Yes?"

Kevin pointed to the window over his shoulder. "What city is that back there?"

"New York," the woman said.

Kevin's jaw dropped. "Yikes!" he said under his breath. "I did it again!"

"Is something wrong?" the woman asked.

Scratching his head, Kevin looked around. There had to be a way out of this. "Where's Florida?" he asked.

The woman pointed to her right. "About a thousand miles that way."

Kevin felt himself go numb. He slowly turned toward the window. Suddenly everything around him looked way too big, way too scary. "Oh, no," he muttered to himself. "My family's in Florida. I'm in New York."

New York? It seemed so far away, a place you only saw on TV. The Big Apple, the City That Never Sleeps, skyscrapers, Radio City Music Hall, the biggest Christmas tree in the world, humongous stores — there it was, rising in the distance like the Emerald City, only dull gray.

And for a short cab ride, he could be there. By himself. With no rules. And with all his dad's money.

Slowly he began to smile. "My family's in Florida . . ." His voice rose to a jubilant shout. "And I'm in New York!"

He whooped with excitement. This could be the chance of a lifetime! Holding tightly to his dad's travel bag, he ran out to the curb. "Cab, please," he said to a uniformed man.

The man didn't even ask questions. He acted as if every ten-year-old boy rode cabs all alone. Maybe they *did* in New York City, Kevin thought.

He already loved the place.

"Where to, pal?" the driver asked.

Good question. Kevin thought a minute, then said, "To where the biggest buildings are."

The driver shot him an annoyed look. "You mean, the World Trade Center?"

"Yeah!"

The cab raced toward the city as if it

were in the Indy 500. Kevin pressed his face to the window in awe. As they zoomed across a bridge, an overhead tram passed them on the right. Beyond it, apartment houses seemed ready to push each other into the river. Further inland was a slant-topped white skyscraper that looked like a gigantic electric razor. And to the left was the Empire State Building, nestled among glass giants that glinted in the bright morning sun. Horns blared around them, choppers slashed across the sky, and a tugboat tooted its lonely horn somewhere in the distance.

No doubt about it. This was definitely the coolest place in the world.

And Kevin McCallister had it all to himself.

In the Miami airport, the McCallister family trudged down to the luggage carousel. Rain pelted the terminal windows. Each time the electric door opened, warm and clammy air gusted in. On the soggy palm trees outside, red-and-green cellophane wreaths sagged with the weight of the downpour.

A tanned man wearing a Santa Claus

outfit with sandals stood by a cauldron, looking at his watch. He halfheartedly rang a small bell and called out in a dull voice, "Christmas is here . . . spread the cheer."

The McCallisters stared silently at the conveyer belt as the first suitcase rolled in. It was the size of a small horse.

"Okay, here it comes," Mrs. McCallister called out. "Everybody takes their own luggage!"

With a grunt, Mr. McCallister hoisted the suitcase off the belt. He read the tag, passed it to his wife, and said, "Give this to Kevin."

She passed it to Uncle Frank, on her right. "Give this to — "

Uncle Frank grimaced. "Uh, I'll have to pass on that, Kate. I have a bad back."

Aunt Leslie took it and gave it to Rod. "Give this to Kevin."

Rod handed it to Megan, on *his* right. "Give this to Kevin."

The suitcase was passed from McCallister to McCallister. The second to the last one was Brooke. "Give this to Kevin," she said, passing it to Fuller.

Fuller turned to his right. An elderly

couple smiled down at him. He looked past them.

No Kevin.

He turned back to Brooke and tapped her on the shoulder. "Kevin's not here."

Brooke took the suitcase and passed it up to Sondra. "Kevin's not here."

As everyone else's bags were passed down the line, Kevin's made its way slowly back up. Aunt Leslie got it from the right just as Mrs. McCallister passed her a suitcase from the left.

"Give this to Buzz," Mrs. McCallister said.

Aunt Leslie exchanged it for Kevin's. "Give this to Peter. Kevin's not here." Then she passed Buzz's suitcase to Rod. "Give this to Buzz."

"Kevin's not here," Mrs. McCallister said automatically as she gave her husband Kevin's suitcase.

Mr. McCallister took the bag and gave his wife a blank look. "What?"

She froze. Her face became taut with panic. Memories of last year came racing back. *"Kevin!"* she screamed.

The McCallisters raced around the airport in a mad rush. They checked everywhere, but there was no sign of Kevin.

Within minutes, they found the airport police office. Mr. McCallister burst in first. "Excuse me, we'd like to report a missing child!"

Behind a steel desk, a burly policeman put down his newspaper. "Have a seat," he said. "And don't worry. This happens from time to time. Never lost one yet." With a reassuring smile, he reached out his hand. "Name's Officer Bennett."

"Peter McCallister," Kevin's dad said, shaking Officer Bennett's hand as he sat down. "My son's name is Kevin."

"Where did you last see him?" Officer Bennett asked.

Mrs. McCallister's face went pale. "Curbside check-in, in Chicago?"

"I saw him when we came in the door at O'Hare," Mr. McCallister said. "He was in the terminal with us."

"Most people get separated at security checkpoints," Officer Bennett said. "Did everyone get through security?"

"I don't know," Mrs. McCallister replied.

"We were in a hurry," her husband said. "We ran all the way to the gate."

Officer Bennett nodded. "When did you notice he was missing?"

"When we picked up our baggage here," Kevin's mom said, turning red with embarrassment.

"Has the boy ever run away from home?" Officer Bennett asked.

"No," said Kevin's dad.

"Has he ever been in a situation where he's been on his own?"

For a moment, no one said a word. Finally Mrs. McCallister said, "Well, as a matter of fact, this has happened to us before." She laughed nervously. "It's becoming a McCallister family travel tradition."

"Funnily enough," Mr. McCallister added with a chuckle, "we never lose our luggage."

Their jokes were met by silence. Mr. and Mrs. McCallister both lost their smiles.

Bowing her head, Kevin's mom said, "He was left home by accident last year."

Officer Bennett's stare became icy cold.

"That is what my wife meant when she said this is a McCallister family travel tradition," Kevin's dad quickly added.

Officer Bennett reached for the telephone. "We'll call Chicago and notify them of the situation. The odds are that's where he is. It's very unlikely he'd be anywhere else."

The McCallister family all exchanged sheepish looks as Officer Bennett called the operator.

Clouds whipped by below Kevin. The spires of midtown skyscrapers seemed far away from where he stood, on the observation deck of the World Trade Center.

Eight million people. That was how many were in New York City, the cab driver had said. Eight million, and every one of them on the streets and in the buildings below Kevin.

"Wow," he said, snapping a picture.

He loved being on top of it all, but he couldn't wait to go down and plunge into the heart of it.

Sticking the camera back in his dad's bag, he headed toward the elevator. He took one last look over his shoulder at the mass of statuesque buildings and teeming streets.

Somewhere in that vast panorama, a battered truck with Illinois license plates snaked through midtown. In its trailer were two men, dressed in poorly fitting clothes.

As Kevin entered the World Trade Center elevator miles away, the van pulled up beside an outdoor market. The trailer door opened and the two men slipped out.

The first man took a deep breath. "Smell that! You know what it is?"

The second man sniffed, then winced. "Yeah, fish."

"No, Marv," the first man said. "It's freedom, and it's money."

Marv shrugged at Harry and sniffed again. "It's freedom . . . and it's fish."

Chapter 6

One thing about being in New York. Even if you were wearing terrible clothes, no one noticed you. That was Harry's first thought as he and Marv rode the subway.

After the prison break, they'd had to ditch their striped convict uniforms. The clothes they found in a local dump weren't too dirty, but they sure didn't fit right.

The train screeched to a stop at a station marked Fifth Avenue. "This is where we score," Harry said. "Let's go."

As they left the car and climbed the stairs, Marv began wrapping tape around his fingers, sticky side out.

Harry's eyes darted right and left. He didn't trust anyone, not in this town. "One quick score, my friend," he said to Marv. "We pick us up a couple of phony passports and we split the country."

They walked to a crowded street corner, where a man in a Santa suit was ringing a bell. Next to him, passersby dropped coins into a metal bucket labeled NEW YORK CHILDREN'S HOSPITAL.

As Harry and Marv walked by him, Marv quickly dipped his hand into the bucket. They walked a few steps more, toward Fifty-ninth Street. Then, beaming with pride, Marv showed his hand to Harry. Coins were stuck to the strips of masking tape around his fingers.

Harry rolled his eyes. "You're really smart, Marv. Bust out of jail, hop a semi, ride seven hundred miles to New York — to swipe fourteen cents off a Santy Claus."

"Every little bit helps," Marv said. "And you know what? Now we got a new name — the Sticky Bandits!"

"That's very cute," Harry said, shaking his head in disgust.

Kevin didn't know how he'd managed to find Central Park, but he was glad he did. What a great place — a zoo, a skating rink, horse-drawn buggies . . .

Just beyond the park's stone fence, a building caught his eye. There were flags flying above the entrance, and pointed towers at the top. He recognized it from Celebrity Ding-Dang-Dong.

"The Plaza Hotel," he said, imitating the TV announcer. "New York's most exciting hotel experience!"

Laughing, he turned back to the park pathway — and stopped dead in his tracks. Ahead of him stood the weirdest thing he'd ever seen.

It looked like a scarecrow with its arms straight out, but it was alive. He couldn't be sure, but it seemed to be an old woman. Pigeons rested along every inch of her arms. They covered her head and shoulders, stuck out of her ragged coat pockets, hung from her skirt.

"Sick," was all Kevin could say. The lady was giving him the creeps. She was like something from a horror movie.

He turned and ran out of the park. Across the street was the Plaza Hotel. It was probably as safe a place as any. No spooky old pigeon lady would follow him there.

He hightailed it to the nearest corner. There was a red light, right above a street sign that said 59TH STREET. The street was jammed with cars, and horns blared like some horrible, angry brass band. When the crowd of pedestrians began to cross, he crossed with them, dodging cars and buses.

On the other side of the street, Harry and Marv began to cross. They weaved around a taxicab, twisting their bodies to avoid the other pedestrians.

It was Harry who saw the familiar blond head of hair, about chest-high. He looked over his shoulder, trying to follow it in the crowd.

Nah, it couldn't be the kid, Harry thought. Not here, hundreds of miles from home.

"What's the matter?" Marv asked.

"I thought I saw something," Harry replied.

Marv turned around to look. Just ahead of him, pedestrians clogged the sidewalk, slowing everyone down. Marv rammed right into the person in front of him.

He turned abruptly around and came face-to-face with a gorgeous, beautifully dressed woman. Marv blushed and smiled. He figured she was a fashion model.

Before he could say a word of apology, she reared back and whacked him across the face.

Just south of Fifty-ninth Street, Kevin walked past a line of limousines, up a set of marble stairs, and into the Plaza Hotel. The lobby took his breath away. Shining marble columns rose to a high, gilded ceiling. People bustled back and forth, speaking every language except English. There were huge restaurants everywhere you looked and indoor shops with fancy names.

"This is great!" he said to himself.

He quickly pulled his Talkboy out of the shoulder bag. He switched tapes, rewound it, and pressed PLAY.

"Guests of the new Celebrity Ding-Dang-Dong stay at the world-renowned Plaza Hotel, New York's most exciting hotel experience. For reservations, call 1-800-759-3000 . . ."

51

Kevin snapped the machine off with a triumphant smile. "I'll do just that," he said.

Snooping around, he found a bank of telephone booths. The phones were way too high, so he grabbed a few phone books from a nearby case and piled them on the floor below the phone.

He climbed up but didn't reach for the phone. There was no way he could just call and make a reservation. The hotel clerks would never take a kid's voice seriously. There had to be another way. He fiddled with the Talkboy, thinking it over.

Of course. The Talkboy! His number-one friend away from home. He lifted the mike close to his mouth and pressed RECORD. In an imitation of his dad's friendly voice, he began talking. "Howdy-do, this is Peter McCallister . . ."

A few moments into his speech, a woman entered the phone booth across from him. She gave Kevin a curious glance.

Kevin leaned out of his booth. "You know," he said, "in the bathrooms they have little toilets for kids. I guess the people who make phone booths don't care as much about kids as the people who make toilets." He shrugged and leaned back into the booth. "Excuse me."

He shut the booth's door and rewound the tape to the beginning of his speech. Then he called the Plaza Hotel.

"Hello, Plaza Hotel reservations, may I help you?" came a voice at the other end.

Kevin held the Talkboy to the mouthpiece and pressed PLAY. "Howdy — " began Kevin's voice. He squeezed the Talkboy with all his strength. He'd done this once before. It slowed down the mechanism, making the voice come out slower and deeper. " — dooooo . . ." Sure enough, the voice suddenly became lower. Kevin sounded like a grown man! "This is Peter McCallister, the father. I'd like to have a hotel room, please. With an extra large bed and a TV and one of those little refrigerators with food in it that you have to open with a key."

Quickly Kevin hit the PAUSE button.

"I'd be happy to arrange that, sir," the reservations clerk said at the other end. "Would you like to leave a credit card number?"

Kevin hit PAUSE again, still squeezing

the Talkboy. "Credit card?" came the low voice. Kevin reached in the shoulder bag for his dad's wallet. "You got it!"

Oops. The "you" in that statement wobbled into Kevin's normal voice as he got out the card. He hoped the clerk didn't notice.

To Kevin's surprise, he heard the clerk say, "Thank you, Mr. McCallister, your room is reserved. Just bring your card with you."

Yeah! Kevin hung up and returned the phone books. Then he peeked over at the reservations desk. Under a sign marked RESERVATIONS, a couple of people were taking phone calls and entering information in a computer.

Kevin thought for a minute. If he went to the people he'd just called, they might be suspicious. But there was another area marked CHECK IN. That was definitely the place to go. The reservation would show on their computer, and they wouldn't know when he had called.

He walked up to the check-in desk. As usual, it was way too high, so he hoisted himself up on his forearms. "Hi," he said to a young woman in a Plaza uniform.

She looked at him distractedly. "May I help you?"

"Reservation for McCallister," Kevin said.

"A reservation . . . for yourself?" she said, narrowing her eyes.

Kevin exhaled, pretending to be impatient. He had his alibi all worked out. "My feet aren't touching the ground. I'm not tall enough to look over this counter. How could I make a reservation for a hotel room? Think about it. A kid coming into a hotel and making a reservation? Not on this planet, ma'am."

"I — I'm confused," the clerk said.

"I'm traveling with my dad," Kevin said. "He's on business. He's at a meeting. I hate meetings, plus I'm not allowed to go in. I can only sit in the lobby, and that's boring. So he dropped me off here." Kevin shifted his weight from one arm to the other, and gave her a Visa card. "He gave me this credit card and said to tell whoever was checking in people to let me in the room, so I don't get into mischief."

The clerk looked at him, then the credit

card. She tapped it in her hand a few times, as if deciding what to do. Then she ran it through a machine and waited. "Well," she said, "it checks out okay." She put the card in an imprint machine and printed out a blank hotel bill with the name *Peter J. McCallister* on it. Then she handed the card back to Kevin and snapped her fingers at a young man in a uniform and cap. "Front, please!"

Kevin looked at the card in amazement. "Wow, it worked!" he said to himself.

"The bellman will assist you," the clerk said as the young man took Kevin's bag. "Enjoy your stay with us. And don't forget to remind your dad, when he arrives, that he has to come down and sign a couple of things."

"My pleasure," Kevin replied. "You've been most helpful."

As he followed the bellman toward the elevator, he could barely keep himself from jumping with joy.

He did it. Now *this* was a vacation!

Behind him, the check-in clerk exchanged a glance with a tall, middle-aged man who was sitting across the lobby at a station marked CONCIERGE. He nodded, as if to say, *Yes, I saw it, too.* Both of them smelled something funny.

Just to be on the safe side, the concierge decided to keep an eye on this young man.

Chapter 7

"All right," Officer Bennett said into his telephone. "Thanks. Merry Christmas."

He looked across his desk. Thirteen grim faces stared back at him. "No sign of your son," he said to Mr. and Mrs. McCallister.

Mrs. McCallister slumped back into her chair. Her husband put his arm around her.

"Do you have a recent photo of the boy?" Officer Bennett asked.

"I have one in my wallet," Mr. McCallister answered. He turned to look for his travel bag, but it wasn't there. His brow began to crease with concern. "I don't have my bag," he said.

"Where did you last see it, Peter?" his wife asked.

He sat back and thought a moment. "Kevin had it at the airport. He was looking for batteries." He shook his head in amazement. "He has my wallet!"

His son was somewhere on this earth with all his money and identification. At least, he hoped that were true. If the bag were to be stolen . . .

"Did you have any credit cards in the wallet?" Officer Bennett asked.

Mr. McCallister nodded. "Credit cards, cash . . ."

"We'll notify the credit card companies immediately," said Officer Bennett. "If your son has the cards, we can get a location on him, when and if he uses them."

"I don't think Kevin even knows how to use a credit card," Mrs. McCallister said.

"Even if he knew," Officer Bennett said, "it's not likely any merchant would let him." He grabbed the receiver from his phone and punched a number. "Hello, this is the Miami Police. I'd like to report a lost credit card and put a tracer on it."

One by one, Officer Bennett made calls to credit-card companies while Mr. and Mrs. McCallister gave him information. It took about a half hour, after which Officer Bennett left to check the missing-persons department.

When he returned, the McCallisters were weary but hopeful.

He shook his head. "No news."

Is good news, Mr. McCallister thought. He relaxed a little. The police always find out the bad stuff first. Maybe this meant Kevin was doing all right.

"If anything develops," Officer Bennett continued, "we're going to have to be able to reach you, so we'd like you to stay here in Miami at least through tonight."

Mr. McCallister looked at his wife and shrugged. "We may as well stay at the hotel. Frank already made reservations for us there."

"Just as long as you leave us with a number and keep a line open," Officer Bennett said.

"Okay," Mrs. McCallister replied, sniffing back a sob. "And . . . thank you for your help."

"Any time, ma'am."

Officer Bennett stood up politely while the McCallister family filed out of his office. He felt bad for them; they all looked so forlorn.

But he felt worse for the poor kid who was lost.

Kevin loved the elevator ride so much, he almost hated to get off. The car was carpeted and wood-paneled, and it had a *sofa*. If there'd been a TV in it, he wouldn't have minded riding up and down all day.

When the door opened, he followed the bellman down a hallway to his room. The bellman opened the door and let Kevin go in first.

"Wow . . ." Kevin said. The place was the size of a house! And outside the window was an incredible view of Central Park. Through the snow-covered trees, he could see ice skaters happily circling the rink. "This is *great*," he said.

He ran into the bedroom. There was a thirty-five-inch TV screen, a cabinet full of videos, a minibar with all kinds of snacks, a small refrigerator, and a king-size bed. He smiled. "A huge bed . . . all for me!"

Kevin yanked open the refrigerator, which was stocked with soda and juice. "How convenient!"

Next stop was the bathroom. Kevin gasped when he opened the door — marble walls, a four-person whirpool tub, a separate shower and bath, and *another* TV. "Luxurious!" Kevin blurted out. "And spacious!"

In the living room, the bellman sneaked a look at the tag on Kevin's bag: *Peter J. McCallister*. He wondered if the bag was stolen. You couldn't trust anyone nowadays, he thought, even a wholesome-looking kid. Especially a wholesome-looking kid on his own in New York City.

Quickly he unzipped the bag and looked inside. A wallet, an envelope —

There were footsteps approaching from the bedroom. The kid was coming back. He zipped up the bag and stood at attention.

"Is the temperature all right for you, sir?" he said as Kevin walked in.

"It's okay," Kevin said.

"Do you know how the TV works?"

"I'm ten years old. TV is my life."

"Of course." The bellman smiled politely. *Smart-aleck kid*, he thought. *I wonder if he knows enough to tip me?* "Do you know that the hotel rents movies? Dial seven-seven and they'll send up a catalog."

"Okay," Kevin said. "Thanks."

"Well . . . ?" the bellman said, hoping Kevin would take a hint.

Kevin looked at him blankly. "What?"

The bellman put out his hand, rubbing his fingers together. *Everyone* knew that meant *tip*, or so he thought.

"Ohhh," Kevin said, nodding with recognition. "I'm sorry."

He reached into his pocket. The bellman smiled.

"Here," Kevin said, pulling out a stick of gum. "And there's plenty more where that came from."

The bellman's smile vanished. He left without saying thank you and slammed the door behind him.

Kevin went to pick up his dad's shoulder bag. Beside it was a card with Plaza phone numbers on it: room service, pool, steam room, movie rental . . .

Kevin's eyes lit up. After a day like this, he was going to have some fun!

He rummaged around in his dad's bag. Next to Bongo, the inflatable clown, he found a pair of swim trunks. He undressed and put on the trunks. The waist was okay when he pulled the drawstring tight, but the pants still billowed out like a skirt.

It looked a little weird, but no matter. He ran into the bathroom, grabbed a Plaza Hotel robe, and scooted out of his room.

The pool was a short elevator ride away. There were a few bored-looking grown-ups there, lounging around on chairs.

"How's the water?" Kevin asked a woman in a bathing suit.

"Nice," she replied.

"Good enough," Kevin said, taking off his robe and walking to the edge of the pool. "Would it bother anyone if I practiced my cannonballs?"

No one answered.

"Thanks," Kevin said. He jumped, tucked in his legs, and hit the water with a loud splash.

Only one person seemed to take any notice of Kevin. Hidden in the shadow of the locker room, the concierge gave him a long, suspicious glance.

After a half hour of swimming, Kevin decided to try the steam room. He spotted a seat through the thick, hot clouds of steam. Sitting down, he could hear two men talking to each other. "Did you see the marketing director at Skilling and Ross? Whoa, is she hot-looking!"

"I know who you're talking about," the other guy said. "She's — "

"Excuse me," Kevin said. "If you guys are going to talk dirty or anything, I'll have to leave. I promised my grandmother I'd never listen to that kind of talk."

Through the swirling steam, Kevin could see their bewildered looks as he walked out.

Kevin felt refreshed when he went back to his room. He sat by the window and watched the sky change color in the setting sun. *Time for dinner,* he thought with a yawn.

Kevin jumped onto the bed and picked up the phone. "Hello, room service, please. . . . Yes, this is Peter McCallister. I'd like to order a deluxe ice-cream sundae. . . . It'll take twenty minutes? Okay, thanks."

Twenty minutes would be enough time for a soak in the hot tub — with a friend, of course. Kevin pulled out Bongo the clown from his dad's bag, brought it to the bathroom, and inflated it.

The tub was great. The clown was actually fun to play with. And the best was yet to come. Wrapped in his dad's robe, Kevin walked back to the bedroom, just as the bell rang.

"Room service!" came a voice from the hallway.

Kevin pulled open the door. "Just in time! Follow me."

He ran into the bedroom. The room-service waiter followed behind him, pushing a cart with containers of ice cream, hot-fudge and butterscotch sauce, and whipped cream.

As the waiter made the sundae, Kevin picked a video out of the cabinet: *Angels with Even Filthier Souls*. He popped it in and plopped on the bed. Soon the waiter left and Kevin was alone with an enormous sundae covered with both sauces.

The actors in the movie were terrible. The music was corny. It was nothing but violence.

Kevin loved it.

He was halfway through eating his sundae when the exciting part began. Carlotta, the gangster's moll, walked into a dark apartment. Outside the window, the lights of the big city twinkled. In the corner was a Christmas tree.

Suddenly she gasped. A dark figure was lurking by the wall. *"Hold it right there!"* came his rough voice.

Carlotta's face showed that she recognized the voice. It was her boyfriend, the toughest mob kingpin in the city.

"I-It's me, Johnny," Carlotta said, trembling.

Johnny turned on a light. His shadow now became a real person — a sinister, slick-haired guy wearing a satin smoking jacket. With an evil smile, he said, *"I knew it was you. I could smell you getting off the elevator."*

"It's gardenias, Johnny," Carlotta said. *"Your favorite."*

"You was here last night, too, wasn't ya?"

"I was singing at the Blue Monkey last night."

Kevin shook his head in disgust. "Yeah, right. Don't listen to her, Johnny."

Johnny snapped, *"You were here smoochin' with my brother."*

"That's a dirty, rotten lie, Johnny," Carlotta insisted. *"My real estate belongs to you."*

"Don't give me that! You been smoochin' with every guy in town — Snuffy, Al, Leo, Little Moe with the gimpy leg, Cheeks, Boney Bob, Cliff. . . . I could go on forever, baby."

"You got me all wrong!" Carlotta's eyes were wide with hysterical fear.

"All right," Johnny said, his voice softening. *"I believe you . . ."*

Leaning over, Johnny pulled something from under the Christmas tree.

Kevin's breath caught in his throat. Johnny was holding a machine gun.

". . . *but my tommy gun don't!*" Johnny said.

"*Johnny, I'm all wool and a yard wide!*" Carlotta pleaded. "*You're the only duck in my pond!*"

"*Get down on your knees and tell me you love me.*"

Carlotta dropped to one knee. "*Baby, I'm over the moon for you!*"

"*You gotta do better than that!*"

"*If my love was an ocean, it would take two airplanes to get across it!*"

Johnny slowly raised his machine gun. "*Maybe I'm off my hinges, but I believe you. That's why I'm gonna let you go.*"

Kevin was getting nervous. He didn't believe Johnny for a minute. "She's rat bait," he said.

"*You got to the count of three to get your lousy, lyin', low-down, four-flushin' carcass out that door. One . . . two . . .*"

With a sudden shriek of laughter, Johnny opened fire. Kevin put his hands over his eyes.

"*Three!*" came Johnny's gravelly voice. "*Merry Christmas, ya two-timin' floozy!*"

When Kevin uncovered his eyes, he saw Carlotta keeled over on the floor. Corny violin music swelled in the background.

Shovelling his sundae into his mouth, Kevin watched the rest of the video. When it ended, he was ready to sack out.

Knock! Knock! Knock!

Kevin bolted out of bed. They've caught on to me, he thought. They're going to come in here, see that there are *still* no grown-ups in the room, and throw me out on the street.

He quickly turned off the lights and ran into the bathroom. He turned the shower on full-blast.

Ding-dong!

In the hallway, the concierge rang the bell once, twice. There was no answer, so either the kid was fast asleep or out of the room.

He grinned. *Now* he'd find out what that little punk was up to. Quietly he opened Kevin's door, using keys he'd gotten from the maid. Peeking inside, he noticed the suite was pitch-dark.

He tiptoed to the bedroom and looked inside, hoping to find the boy's suitcase. The bathroom door was ajar and the shower was running. He peered in.

Through the fogged glass of the shower

stall, the concierge could see a tall, beefy man doing a dance and singing. He recognized the song: "Cool Jerk."

The concierge backed away, but it was too late. The man stopped dancing. "Hey, get out of here, you nosy little creep!" he shouted in a deep, angry voice. "Or I'll come out and slap you silly!"

Mortified, the concierge backed away. He turned and ran out of the suite, banging his knee on a chair.

As he hobbled down the hallway, he felt waves of pain, anger, and shame. He could have sworn no adult had checked into that room.

There was something very strange going on here — and he wasn't going to stop until he found out what.

Chapter 8

Kevin laughed out loud. He clicked off his Talkboy. His trick had worked.

He stood up from his hiding place next to the bathroom sink. The three strings in his hands went slack — the strings that had been attached to the head and arms of Bongo the clown. Kevin had propped him up in the shower, draped the strings over the top of the shower door, and moved the clown like a marionette. Fogged over by the shower's steam, Bongo must have looked like a real person.

And, thanks to his Talkboy, he'd had a perfect recording of Uncle Frank's voice.

Kevin ran out of the bathroom, all the

way to the front door. Whoever had come in hadn't left a trace. Oh, well, it was probably some Plaza employee, snooping around to see if there was an adult in the room. Now he knew — there *was*.

He just didn't know the adult was Bongo the clown.

In a dreary roadside motel in Miami, the McCallisters unpacked. Outside, the motel's sign hung lopsided in the rain, about to fall down. An old car sat up on blocks, surrounded by dead palm trees on the muddy lawn.

Mr. McCallister grumbled as he passed Uncle Frank on his way to the motel office. "Couldn't you do better than this?"

Uncle Frank shrugged. "It didn't look this bad on our honeymoon."

Gloomily the other McCallisters unpacked in their rooms. They had all felt terrible the year before, when they'd left Kevin behind. But stranding him in an airport somehow seemed worse.

Even Buzz had stopped being his usual rowdy self. In his room, Buzz sat silent and slump-shouldered on a cheap motel chair. As he stared listlessly out the window, his brother Jeff tried to talk to him.

"Buzz?"

Buzz didn't move. "What?"

"You're really upset, huh?" *That* was an understatement. Jeff had never seen his brother so quiet.

"Very," Buzz replied, his voice barely audible.

"Are you . . . crying?"

"Not yet."

Jeff sat on the side of the bed nearest his brother. "It's not your fault Kevin's gone," he said gently. "We're all lousy to him. But it's going to be okay. He's a tough little guy. He'll make it, wherever he is. Try to get some sleep. You'll go nuts staring out the window like that."

Buzz nodded, but just kept on staring.

The poor guy was beyond help, Jeff thought. He probably needed to deal with his feelings alone. With a sigh, Jeff lay down to go to sleep.

A smile formed on Buzz's face. His eyes began to light up. There she was, in the window, walking through her motel room in the opposite wing. She was just as beautiful as the first time he spotted her.

He knew if he kept looking long enough, she'd come back.

Somewhere in the back of his mind, he knew that Jeff had asked him something, but he couldn't remember what it was.

Oh, well, it probably didn't matter.

The first thing Kevin had noticed about New York nights was that they weren't really *dark*. Outside his window, he saw that the streetlights cast everything in a kind of dull amber.

Except in Central Park. There were streetlights there, too, but they just dotted the park along some of the roads. Between the lights was nothing but inky blackness. Who knew what went on in there? Seeing that spooky pigeon lady was bad enough — and that was in broad daylight!

Kevin shuddered. You'd have to be insane to go in there at night, he thought. The Plaza was definitely the place to be.

As he settled back into bed, he caught a glimpse of his ice cream sundae bowl. It was empty except for a puddle of brown glop at the bottom. He had never tasted anything so good. "Sinful," his mom would have called it, shaking her head — but she would have eaten one herself, no problem. And so would his dad.

Kevin smiled at the thought of his parents. They would have loved it in New York. His mom would have gone crazy over the room, his dad would have wanted to spend the whole day walking around.

This was the place they should have booked for vacation — not stupid old Florida. If the Plaza was too expensive, they could have stayed with Uncle Rob.

Kevin sat up. He'd almost forgotten about Uncle Rob. Kevin's dad said that Uncle Rob owned a whole brownstone in New York — whatever *that* meant.

He reached into the suitcase and pulled out his dad's address book. Flipping to the *M*'s, he saw

McCALLISTER, ROB
51 West 95th Street
New York, New York 10025

Kevin's dad had said Uncle Rob had taken his family to Paris. But he hadn't mentioned when they were coming home.

"Hm," Kevin said to himself. "If they're back, I'll drop in on them. They usually give pretty good presents."

He put back the address book and pulled out his dad's wallet. A corner of a snapshot peeked from it. Kevin took it out.

He remembered it well. It was Thanksgiving Day. Buzz was choking him and Jeff was making rabbit ears behind his mom's head. His dad had his arms around Megan and Linnie, and he was trying to smile. Problem was, Megan was blowing a bubble and Linnie was scratching her leg, which made his dad look totally dorky.

Kevin couldn't help grinning. Typical McCallister pose.

From the street came a jingling sound. He looked out to see a horse-drawn carriage pull away from the curb. Inside the carriage was a family, snuggled happily under thick blankets and singing carols.

A few blocks beyond them, a giant Christmas star shone on top of a building. It looked as if it were about to rise to the heavens.

Kevin felt his stomach sink — and he

knew it wasn't the sundae. New York was great, fantastic, a dream. But right then, all he could think about was his family.

By now they knew he was gone. Did they miss him? Were they worried?

Maybe they thought he'd missed the plane and gone home. Maybe they were home now, looking for him!

Kevin ran to the phone and punched out his number. His heart raced as he waited for an answer.

Mrs. McCallister felt as soggy as the warm rain that fell outside. The Christmas tree in her motel room was made of dusty plastic, and there was a battered tin star at the top.

Somehow, the holiday spirit escaped her.

She couldn't stop thinking about Kevin. Was he in Miami? Did he fall asleep on the plane and forget to get off? Did he get on the wrong plane in Chicago? Did he miss the plane and go home?

She sat up with a start. Of course! That was probably what happened.

Shaking nervously, she dialed her home number. It rang once . . . twice . . .

At about the tenth time, she gave up hope and hung up.

In the McCallister house, two lights blinked on their four-line phone for a few moments. One of them went out when Mrs. McCallister hung up.

The other went out, too, when Kevin McCallister put down the receiver at the Plaza Hotel.

Chapter 9

Ding-dong!

Kevin fell out of bed. His eyes blinked. Sunlight was streaming into his room. For a split second he wondered how his dad managed to install a new carpet while he was asleep.

Then he remembered. The Plaza Hotel. New York. Doorbell.

"Coming!" Kevin picked up his Plaza robe from the floor, put it on, and ran to the door.

"Good morning," said the bellman as Kevin yanked the door open. In his right hand he held out a pair of freshly laundered underpants, pinned to a hanger and covered with plastic. "Your drawers, sir."

Kevin snatched them out of his hands. "Hey, don't flash these babies around!" Kevin said, glancing up and down the empty hall. "There could be girls on this floor."

"Uh, I was very careful, sir," the bellman said.

"When it comes to underwear," Kevin replied, "you can never be too careful."

The bellman gave Kevin a wan smile.

Now, Kevin had been in the city long enough to catch on to a few rules of the trade. Never forget to take care of the help, that was an important one. Reaching into his robe pocket, he pulled out a stick of gum and handed it to the bellman.

"Thank you, sir," the bellman said dryly.

Kevin closed the door. All his fear and sadness from the night before had disappeared. With fresh underwear and a good night's sleep, he felt just about ready to face his first full day in New York City.

But first, a shower and shave. After all, no seasoned traveler would dare leave his hotel without that!

Whistling, Kevin skipped into the bathroom and stood for a long time under the shower's warm, refreshing stream. Then, wrapping himself in his complimentary bath towel, he stood by the sink and flicked on his complimentary electric razor. He shaved carefully, felt the remarkable smoothness of his cheeks, and combed his hair with his complimentary comb.

"I'm not entirely crazy about vacationing alone," Kevin said to his mirror image, "especially somewhere where I've never been and nobody knows me. But since I can't call my parents because they're not home and I don't know what number they're at, I'll just have to make the best of the situation."

On the shelf below the mirror, Kevin saw a bottle marked COMPLIMENTARY AFTER-SHAVE. He picked it up, unscrewed the cap, and sniffed it.

Not bad. Sort of limey. "I think I'm old enough for this stuff now," he said. A year ago, he had tried some and it stung like crazy. But he was just a kid then. Not a seasoned traveler.

He splashed some after-shave onto his

palm. He rubbed his hands together, then slapped them to his cheeks.

Kevin froze. The color drained from his face. In the mirror, he could see his mouth falling open in a silent gape of pain.

"AAAAAAAAAAGGGHHHHHH!"

A few moments later, Kevin had calmed down. His cheeks had lost their fiery redness. It no longer felt as if they'd been scraped by sandpaper and doused with lemon juice.

And he'd found a number for a limousine service right near the hotel phone. All expenses conveniently chargeable to his Plaza bill.

Kevin slung his backpack over his shoulder. Then he took his dad's cash envelope from the travel bag, stuffed it in his pocket, and went down to the lobby.

Strolling up to the concierge's desk, he asked, "Is my transportation here?"

The concierge nodded. "Out in front, sir. A limousine and a pizza. And, by the way, they're compliments of the Plaza Hotel."

"New York's most exciting hotel experience," Kevin said.

"I do hope your father understands that last night I was simply checking the room to make sure everything was in order," the concierge said with a toothy smile.

So *he* was the one who was snooping around the night before, Kevin realized. No wonder the limo was free. The concierge must have felt guilty.

"Well, he was pretty mad," Kevin said. "He said he didn't come all the way to New York to get his naked rear end spied on."

"Of course not. Will he be down soon?"

"He already left."

The concierge frowned. "I would have liked to offer my personal apology."

"If some guy looked at you in the shower, would you want to see him ever again?" Kevin asked.

"I suppose not."

Kevin shook his head. "I don't think you'll see him for the rest of our trip."

"I understand," the concierge said solemnly.

"Bye."

The concierge smiled stiffly. "Have a pleasant day."

Kevin bounded away, pushing his way

through the Plaza's revolving doors. As he stepped outside, he looked around eagerly for his ride.

He didn't have to look far. It was parked right in front of the Plaza. And it was the longest, shiniest, *whitest* vehicle he'd ever seen. The driver and a Plaza doorman stood beside it, looking straight at Kevin. Through the open rear door came the smell of fresh, hot pizza.

Kevin just stood there, his mouth hanging open. It was so . . . so *big*. It had to be someone else's limo. The driver and doorman chuckled at Kevin's reaction, and the driver gestured for him to enter.

Slowly Kevin began to grin. "Buzz," he said under his breath, "if you could see me now."

He ran down the Plaza steps and practically dove into the limo. Picking up a steaming-hot slice of extra cheese pizza, he called to the driver, "Take me to the biggest toy store in town."

"You got it," the driver called back.

The limo pulled away from the curb, and Kevin thought, *This must be what it's like in heaven.*

* * *

Behind the Plaza check-in desk, the concierge flipped through the hotel's room records.

Mansfield, Marshall, Mays . . .

Yes, he had heard the man in the shower. Yes, he had seen the outline of someone quite tall. But none of the check-in staff had seen anyone besides the kid enter or leave. Maybe the kid had pulled some sort of practical joke.

McArdle, McBurney . . .

There it was: *McCallister, Peter J.* He pulled out the credit card slip and went to the electronic approval machine.

Carefully he punched in the card's number and waited. The machine burbled and clicked, and its little screen went blank.

Finally, in bright green letters, a word flashed in front of his eyes:

STOLEN

Chapter 10

"Get out of here!" Harry picked up his newspaper and stomped his feet angrily. A group of pigeons lazily turned and walked away from him.

Harry hated pigeons. Rats with wings, he called them. They didn't know how to leave a guy in peace.

He went back to his newspaper. There had to be a clue in there — an ad, an article, *some place* that looked easy to rob. . . .

Ice skaters whizzed by, but only Marv seemed to notice them. It was a bright, crisp day at the Wollman Rink in Central Park, and the ice was already crowded.

While Harry sat back on the park bench, Marv was leaning forward, his eyes darting around.

A little boy came skating toward them. His hands were bare, his mittens dangling out of each coat sleeve. He rocked from side to side, coming closer . . . closer . . .

At the precise moment, Marv reached out and grabbed the boy's mitten. The boy kept going, but the mitten didn't. It came right out of the sleeve, with a piece of yarn attached. The yarn kept coming and coming, turning the boy around, then . . . *zip!* Out popped the other mitten.

Marv gathered up the mittens and yarn, and he gave them to Harry. "Mittens?" he asked.

"You want to knock it off, Marv?" Harry said, angrily putting his paper down.

"They're wool," Marv said admiringly.

"Never mind the mittens!" Harry retorted.

Marv shrugged and put them in his coat pocket.

"We got to face facts," Harry went on. "We don't have the equipment to pull off anything big — your banks, your jewelry stores . . ."

"Your art museums," Marv added.

"Right. We don't want goods, because we don't have the connections here yet to hide anything. We need cash and we need it now."

A girl skated by, wearing a long scarf. Marv reached out again. He grabbed the scarf tightly.

The girl fell to the ice. With a giggle, Marv stuffed her scarf into his pocket.

"How about the hotels?" Marv suggested. "Tourists carry cash."

Harry shook his head. "No guarantees. I got a better idea. It's Christmas Eve, right? People do a lot of shopping today. But the stores ain't going to take their money to the banks because the banks are closed, right?"

"Yeah," Marv said. "So the money stays in the stores overnight!"

"Now, at the expensive joints, customers mostly use credit cards. So the stores that'll have the most cash on hand are the ones that trade in moderate-priced goods."

"Right."

"What store is going to do the most cash business at Christmas time that nobody's going to think to rob?"

Marv thought a moment. "Liquor store?"

"Come on, Marv! *Kids* rob liquor stores." He folded his newspaper and held it toward Marv. "This is what I had in mind."

Marv squinted at a large advertisement for a store called Duncan's Toy Chest. The ad was a busy swirl of bicycles, video games, dolls, and action figures.

"Brilliant, Harry," Marv said with a grin.

"There's nobody dumb enough to knock off a toy store on Christmas Eve," Harry said.

Marv gave Harry a sly, knowing look. "Oh, yes, there is."

On a street not far from the Plaza, Kevin's driver pulled his limo to the curb. He hopped out and ran around to open Kevin's door. "Here we are, sir," he said.

Kevin stepped out onto the bustling sidewalk. His eyes were glued to the store that loomed over him. He had never imagined a toy store this big. No, that wasn't the whole truth. He had never imagined *any* store this big. It must have been seven stories high and a full block wide.

The front window didn't look like a display, it looked like a whole city of toys. Train tracks snaked around piles of games, all flecked with fake snow. Whistling and chugging away, miniature railroad cars passed miniature people, who waved in response. A Santa flew above it all, driving eight reindeer with kicking legs. Christmas carols tinkled loudly in the background, and lights blinked in the windows of dozens of tiny houses.

Over the front door was a huge, mechanical toy chest that opened and closed, revealing animated toys inside. On the chest, surrounded by brightly colored lights, were the words DUNCAN'S TOY CHEST.

Kevin could barely speak. "Merry Christmas, Kevin," he whispered to himself.

The driver shut Kevin's door. "When shall I come back for you, sir?" he called out.

"What time is it now?" Kevin asked.

"Nine-thirty," the driver replied.

"Um . . . how about three o'clock?"

"Three?" The driver raised his eyebrows in surprise. "That's five and a half hours."

Kevin thought it over. "Okay," he said. "Make it three-thirty."

"Yes, sir," the driver said. He climbed back into the limo and drove away.

Kevin unlocked his eyes from the window. He elbowed his way through the throng of shoppers and barged inside.

If the window was like a city of toys, the store itself was a galaxy, a *universe* of pleasure. Kevin had to stand still to take it all in. Wherever he looked — walls, ceilings, floors — there was something he wanted. A radio-controlled plane whizzed from one end of the store to the other, boats floated around in water tanks, a popcorn machine rat-tat-tatted away next to an old-fashioned ice-cream parlor. Kids were playing with demonstration toys, and the salespeople weren't even yelling at them. In fact, they were all *smiling*!

Kevin felt so high, he thought his feet

would leave the ground. "This is the greatest accident of my life," he muttered to himself.

Then, wasting no time, he plunged into the action. He grabbed a pair of pistols from a display counter, shoved a helmet over his head, and whooped at the top of his lungs. Near the counter was a trampoline, so Kevin jumped right on it. He bounced up and down, screaming with joy.

At the top of each jump, he seemed to hover in the air. That was his favorite part. And considering the way he was feeling, he wouldn't have been surprised if he never came down.

On the second floor of Duncan's Toy Chest, in a quiet section marked OUTDOOR PLAYHOUSES, two kid-sized, wooden-shingle houses stood side by side. At once, both front doors slowly opened. Harry and Marv peered out, looking cautiously around.

"Nice house," Marv commented as he stepped out, "but no bathroom."

"Perfect hiding places," Harry said. "Everybody leaves for a nice holiday off, we come out of our little houses and empty the cash registers. We turn off the burglar alarm and walk out like we own the joint."

"Too bad we can't take the houses. We'll need a place to live."

"Will you come on?" Harry said, walking away. "Let's get out of this place before anyone gets suspicious."

They took the escalator down, into the mass of shrieking kids on the first floor. Harry was definitely looking forward to the nighttime hours.

Silent niiiiight . . .

Harry smiled when he heard the familiar carol. The real silent night was only a few hours away. He couldn't wait.

Chapter 11

A bag of mini-robots. A bottle of Monster Sap Super Slippery Bath Bubbles. A deluxe stainless steel jackknife. A Game Gear. A couple of game cartridges.

Kevin loaded each item onto the checkout counter. He would have chosen more, but this was about all he could carry.

"Are you shopping alone?" asked the old man behind the cash register.

"In New York?" Kevin replied, as if the question were incredibly silly. "Sir, I'm afraid of my own shadow."

The old man laughed. His belly jiggled beneath his neat, three-piece suit. "Well, I like to check."

"That's very responsible of you."

"Thank you."

"My pleasure."

The man's fingers tapped out the prices on the cash register. "That'll be twenty-three dollars and seventy-five cents."

Kevin pulled his dad's cash envelope out of his pocket. He took out two twenty-dollar bills and handed them to the man.

"Oh, my," the man said. "Where did you get all that money?"

Kevin thought quickly. "I . . . have a lot of grandmothers."

The old man nodded as he put Kevin's things in a bag.

"You have a really nice store here," Kevin said, changing the subject. "One of the finer toy dealerships I've visited in my life."

"Thank you," the old man replied.

"This Mr. Duncan must be a pretty nice guy to let kids come in his store and play with the toys. Most toy stores prohibit that, you know."

"Is that so?"

"Yep."

"Well, Mr. Duncan loves kids. As a matter of fact, all the money the store takes in today, he donates to the Children's Hospital. The day after Christmas, we total up all the money in the cash registers and Mr. Duncan takes it down to the hospital."

"That's very generous of him," Kevin said.

"Children bring him a lot of joy," the old man said, handing Kevin his bag, "as they do for anyone who appreciates them."

Kevin took the bag and turned to leave. But he couldn't help thinking of the Children's Hospital. Imagine what it must be like to be there on Christmas, he thought. Surrounded by sad and sick kids, away from home and family . . .

He stopped. Reaching into the envelope, he pulled out another twenty. He turned back to the old man. "I'm not supposed to spend this money, but I have twenty dollars from shoveling snow in a jar in our garage where my older brother can't find it, and I can pay my mother back with that." Kevin held out the money to the elderly cashier. "So you can give this to Mr. Duncan. The hospital needs it more than me because I'll probably just spend it on stuff that rots my teeth and my mind."

"That's very sweet of you," the man replied with a grateful smile. As he took the money, he gestured to something behind Kevin. "Now, you see that Christmas tree right there?"

Kevin turned. The tree was only a couple of feet high, but it was dazzling. Among the glittering lights were tiny, handcrafted figurines. A music box played the song "The Twelve Days of Christmas," and Kevin realized the figurines were the objects of that song. There were twelve lords a-leaping, eleven pipers piping (or something like that) . . .

"In appreciation of your generosity," the old man said, "I'm going to let you select an object from that tree to take with you."

"For free?" Kevin said, amazed.

"Yes, sir. May I make a suggestion?"

"Okay."

"Take the two turtledoves."

"I can have *two*?"

The old man nodded. "Two turtledoves, and I'll tell you what you do. You keep one and you give the other one to a person who's very special to you. Turtledoves are a symbol of friendship and love. So long as the two of you have your turtledoves, you'll be friends no matter how far away you might be. Even if you never see each other again, so long as you have the turtledoves, you'll be friends."

"Wow," Kevin said. "I didn't know that. I thought they were just part of a song."

"They are," the old man replied, "and for a reason."

Kevin plucked the two turtledoves off the tree. They really were cool-looking, with incredible detail. And who knew? After what the old man had said, they might even come in handy someday. He put them in his pocket and took his shopping bag from the counter. "Thanks!"

"Merry Christmas," the man said.

"Merry Christmas to you, too. Be sure and bundle up when you go outside. It's a little nippy."

The old man smiled again. He and Kevin waved good-bye.

Clutching his bag, Kevin walked toward the front door. Beside it was a shelf full of pamphlets and maps. Kevin took a sightseeing map of New York and put it in his bag. Just before he passed through the door, he caught a glimpse of a large portrait above it. There was a name carved in brass underneath the portrait: E. F. DUNCAN.

Kevin glanced upward and stopped short.

The hair was a little darker, the belly a little smaller — but other than that, the man in the picture was a dead ringer for the old cashier.

Kevin spun around to look at the man again, but he was gone.

Just before he and Harry got to the second-floor stairs, Marv stopped at a display table. There was a stack of long, hairy gorilla arms, with pink rubber fingertips. He put one on and fiddled around with the controls inside. The fingers began moving around. Giggling, Marv tucked the forearm into his coat sleeve.

"Harry, check it out," he called out.

When Harry turned around, Marv held up the arm and gnashed his teeth.

"Come on, egghead, quit messing around," Harry said.

"This might be nice for picking pockets."

"Put it down!"

"Watch. I'll pick my own pocket."

Harry shook his head. "You're really a moron, you know that?"

Marv reached behind him. He twisted his arm around, trying to reach for his own back pants pocket. It was harder than he expected, without being able to see what he was doing.

There was something else he didn't see — a crowd of shoppers right behind him. As the gorilla paw groped around, its fingers caught on the hem of a skirt.

Unfortunately for Marv, the skirt was on a living human being.

And this human being was not amused.

With a gasp, she whirled around to see the hairy paw. Marv whirled around, too. He was just as surprised as she was — especially when he saw her face.

He knew who she was. In fact, just the previous day, *she'd* been the one who had slapped him in the face as he crossed the street.

Marv just stared, too numb and embarrassed to say a word.

The woman grabbed the toy arm. She reached into it and pulled the levers. The paw's index and middle fingers jutted straight out.

Then she jabbed Marv firmly in his dumbstruck face.

It was three-twenty when Kevin stepped out of the store. The limo was due in ten minutes. He slipped his purchases into his backpack, keeping out the jackknife and the sightseeing map.

The knife was thick with different attachments. He pulled out a nail file, a corkscrew, a small can opener . . .

Ah, there it was. A magnifying glass.

Looking through the lens, he inspected the map. Along the side were photos and drawings of different sights. He paused at each one.

Behind him, the store's front door swung open. Out came Harry and Marv, squinting in the afternoon sunlight.

Harry looked up and down the street. His eyes stopped when he saw Kevin's backpack.

The name *McCallister* was stenciled on a strip of canvas across the top.

Harry began to grin. His face brightened with the purest, most evil sense of victory. The rays of the sun glinted against a silver tooth cap he'd gotten in prison.

Like a mirror, the shiny cap reflected the sun. It sent a pinpoint beam of strong, white light through Kevin's magnifying glass.

The lens strengthened the light, made it brighter and hotter. It landed on the photo Kevin was studying.

Kevin admired the picture of the Statue of Liberty. Especially the realistic torch. It looked as though it actually were glowing . . .

When it burst into real flames, Kevin dropped the map. He jumped back and caught sight of two people standing behind him.

He spun around. His breath caught in his throat.

The two bandits smiled back at him. Harry's tooth still shone brightly.

"Hiya, pal," said Harry.

Chapter 12

"Aaaaaaaaahhh!"

Kevin couldn't hold back a scream. He tore off down the street.

Startled pedestrians turned to look. Harry and Marv laughed pleasantly, trying to look like two uncles whose nephew was being mischievous.

Then they sped after him.

The sidewalks were clogged. People bumped into each other as they trundled along, laden with packages and bags.

Kevin weaved among the crowd, dodging between the shoppers. He reached the street corner and ran into the stopped traffic on Madison Avenue. As he zig-zagged between cars, horns trumpeted in his ears.

Harry and Marv lost him at the corner. Marv hoisted himself onto a street lamp. He looked up and down the street.

A shock of bouncing blond hair was making its way to the opposite curb.

"There he is!" Marv shouted, pointing in Kevin's direction.

The two men tromped across Madison Avenue, squeezing between the cars.

Kevin's blood pulsed with the rhythm of his feet pounding the pavement. He turned onto a side street. There were fewer people there, and he picked up speed. He sprinted around a street vendor's table, loaded with jewelry and trinkets on display.

"Necklaces . . . bracelets . . . presents for mother . . ." the man chanted.

Kevin stopped. An idea had forced its way through the panic in his brain. He pulled a few bills from his pocket. "Those," he said breathlessly, pointing to a pile of beaded necklaces.

The man handed him a half dozen of

them, and Kevin tore off again. He could hear Harry and Marv's footsteps behind him.

The next street was Fifth Avenue, which bordered Central Park. He crossed the street and ran south, following the park's eastern stone wall. Just ahead, beyond the corner of the park, he could see the Plaza Hotel.

But Kevin wasn't going into the hotel. Not yet. First he had to throw Harry and Marv off the trail.

He turned right on Fifty-ninth Street. Now he was running along the park's southern wall. As he ran, his hands pulled at the necklaces. The strings were stronger than he had expected. They didn't seem to want to give. Soon Kevin was plunging blindly across Sixth Avenue, yanking as hard as he could. Cars screeched to a stop, swerving around him.

Finally, in the middle of the street, the necklaces exploded in a cascade of shining, round beads. They spilled onto the street, rolling and bouncing.

Kevin hopped onto the opposite curb. He cast a lightning-quick glance over his shoulder.

Harry and Marv were a few yards behind him. They ran onto Sixth Avenue. Their eyes were trained on Kevin; their teeth gritted with determination.

And their feet were headed right for the spilled beads.

"Whoooooooaaaaa!" In an instant the two men weren't running anymore. They were flying. Their arms flailed helplessly as they somersaulted through the air.

By the time they landed on their backs in the street, Kevin was heading back toward the Plaza Hotel. He ran down the opposite side of Fifty-ninth, sidestepping more pedestrians. It was hard to pick up speed. He hoped that Harry and Marv didn't see him.

The Plaza bordered on Fifty-ninth Street, but its entrance was around the corner to the right. Kevin could see the back of a line of taxis that stretched all the way from the hotel entrance to the street.

His old friend, the concierge, was loading a well-dressed couple into the last cab. As Kevin reached the corner, the concierge turned and saw him. With a stern face, he stepped directly into Kevin's path.

Kevin stopped, panting for breath. He desperately wanted to turn the corner and get out of Harry and Marv's line of sight. "There's .. two guys . . ." he said, gulping air and pointing toward Sixth Avenue.

The concierge's brow formed an angry ledge over his eyes. Without warning, he reached into Kevin's pocket.

"Hey!" Kevin protested.

"What's the matter?" the concierge said. "The store wouldn't take your — " He yanked out Kevin's credit card and envelope full of cash. " — *stolen* credit card?"

Kevin froze. The concierge grabbed him by the collar.

Struggling to get loose, Kevin turned toward Sixth Avenue. There, through a break in the traffic, he could see Harry rubbing his neck in pain.

And staring straight at him.

Chapter 13

Kevin struggled, but the concierge's grip was strong. Finally, with a burst of strength, Kevin broke loose. The concierge leaped after him, but Kevin made tracks toward the hotel.

He flew up the stairs and into the lobby. Behind him, the concierge's voice shattered the muffled conversations of the hotel guests.

"Stop that child!"

All eyes turned to Kevin. People in the glass-walled restaurant dropped their silverware. There was a scream of shock.

As Kevin ran past the front desk, he saw the check-in clerk ducking out a back door. When Kevin rounded the corner to get to the elevators, he saw her again.

She was blocking the elevator door. It slid open, as if beckoning Kevin to enter. As Kevin ran closer, the woman reached out to grab him.

He's rounding third and coming home, a voice shouted in Kevin's head. *It's going to be close. The catcher's blocking the plate . . .*

Kevin slid, feet-first.

He slides . . .

On the slick marble floor, he sailed under her legs.

He scores!

Kevin scrambled to his feet and hopped into an elevator. He turned to see the clerk staring at him in astonishment.

The sound of stomping footfalls made her turn around. Holding her hands out in front of her, she let out a terrified scream.

It was too late. The concierge and the bellman tried to slow down, but they had too much momentum.

Kevin winced. With a loud thud, the two men plowed into the clerk. All three tumbled to the floor.

The elevator door whooshed quietly closed. Kevin exhaled deeply, then pressed FOUR.

As the elevator rose, Kevin's mind was crowded with thoughts. But somehow one thought stuck out. The concierge had accused him of having a stolen credit card. And really, when you thought about it, he was right.

Kevin slumped against the elevator's back wall. "I've committed credit card fraud!"

Harry and Marv limped down Fifty-ninth Street. A bruise was already forming on Marv's face. Harry's pants were ripped and filthy.

"We lost him," Marv moaned.

"We didn't lose him," Harry retorted. "He went in the hotel. And when he comes out — *wham*, we'll get him!"

"What about his folks?"

Harry grinned. "He ain't with his folks."

"How do you know?"

"How do I know?" Harry snorted at the stupidity of that question. "The kid was *alone!*"

Marv nodded. Massaging his aching head, he walked with Harry to the Plaza Hotel.

As long as it took, they would wait.

When the elevator opened on the fourth floor, Kevin dashed down the hall and into his suite. He ran through the living room and straight into the bedroom. There he picked up his travel bag and dumped everything out on the bed. His airplane ticket floated to the bedspread.

Kevin grabbed the ticket and read it. It was his return trip to Chicago! He could probably use it at the New York airport.

"I've had enough of this vacation," he declared. "I'm going home."

Quickly he began loading his backpack — toothbrush, Polaroid camera, and just a few other essentials. If he had to make a getaway, he might as well travel light.

His ears perked up. Outside he could hear the swooshing of the elevator door and the clatter of running feet.

No time to panic. He did the first thing that came to mind.

Reaching into the video cabinet, he took

out *Angels with Even Filthier Souls*. In one swift motion he shoved it into the VCR, then flicked on the TV. He kept his finger on the volume, cranking it up to full.

Crassssh! Just outside the bedroom, in the suite's living room, the front door burst open.

The television crackled to life. An image of a darkened room came on the screen. It was a familiar scene, exactly the one Kevin wanted.

"Hold it right there!" came the rough voice of Johnny the gangster.

Kevin pressed MUTE on the remote. A frightened Carlotta moved her lips but said nothing.

The noise in the living room stopped. "This is the concierge, sir," came a firm but hesitant voice.

Kevin glanced toward the half-open bedroom door. Good. He couldn't see the people in the living room. That meant they couldn't see him. He pressed the MUTE button again. The sound toggled on again, just as Johnny was stepping out of the shadows. *"I knew it was you,"* he said. *"I could smell you getting off the elevator."*

113

Kevin pressed MUTE for Carlotta's response, then pressed it again. *"You were here last night, too, wasn't ya?"*

The concierge cleared his throat. "Uh . . . yes, sir, I was."

Kevin was getting to be an expert at shutting out everything but Johnny's angry voice. *"You were here smoochin' with my brother."*

Oops.

"You — you must be mistaken, sir!" came the concierge's shocked response.

"Don't give me that! You been smoochin' with every guy in town — Snuffy, Al, Leo, Little Moe with the gimpy leg, Cheeks, Boney Bob, Cliff. . . . I could go on forever, baby."

Kevin could barely stifle a laugh. He was dying to see the concierge's face.

If he could, he would have seen it go suddenly white. The concierge stood dumbstruck in the middle of the room, flanked by the bellman and the clerk. Behind them stood two burly security guards. One of the guards looked mortified.

The bellman sneaked a look at the guard's name tag.

Cliff.

"I'm terribly sorry, sir, but you're mistaken," the concierge said, his voice trembling. "We're looking for a young man — "

Johnny's voice cut him off. *"All right, I believe you . . ."*

The concierge relaxed a little.

". . . but my tommy gun don't!"

Five pairs of eyes went wide with disbelief in the living room.

"Get down on your knees and tell me you love me."

Kevin fast-forwarded to Johnny's next line, then pressed PAUSE.

In the next room, the concierge wiped beads of cold sweat from his forehead. "All of us, sir? Or just me?"

There was no answer. Just to be safe, he turned to the others and commanded, "On your knees!" Then, in a timid voice, he called out to the bedroom, "I love you!"

The bellman wiped his brow. "Me, too," he mumbled.

Kevin pressed PAUSE again, and Johnny snapped, *"You gotta do better than that!"*

From the living room, all the voices answered, "I love you."

Kevin stifled a giggle. He quietly put on his coat and his backpack, stuffed his coat pockets with bags of Doritos from the minibar, and clipped the Talkboy onto his belt. At the last minute, he stuffed some Plaza stationery in his pack — a souvenir.

Holding his ticket firmly, he tiptoed to the other end of the bedroom. There was a back doorway there, and Kevin pushed his way through.

As he walked into the hallway, he could hear Johnny saying, *"Maybe I'm off my hinges, but I believe you. That's why I'm gonna let you go."*

Kevin shut the door without a click, ran down the hall, and ducked into the hotel stairwell. He kept the stairwell door open a crack and peeked through. No way was he going to miss the ending of this.

Inside his living room, the concierge and his cohorts shuffled to their feet. They looked at each other with half-smiles, embarrassed but relieved.

"You got to the count of three to get your

lousy, lyin', low-down, four-flushin' car-cass out that door!"

In a mad scramble, they all rushed for the entrance.

"One . . . two . . ."

Clawing each other to get through first, the five of them tumbled out the door. As they ran for their lives, hotel guests peered out of their doors in horror.

RAT-A-TAT-A-TAT-A-TAT-A-TAT-A-TAT-A-TAT . . .

Johnny's wild cackle echoed through the fourth-floor hallway over the sound of machine gun fire. *"Three!"* his murderous voice rang out.

Kevin mouthed the last words of the scene along with Johnny: *"Merry Christmas, ya two-timin' floozy!"*

With a grin of triumph, Kevin disappeared down the stairs. At the first floor, he ran out into a dingy corridor. There were trash bags and cleaning materials along the walls, and at the end, an open garage-type door.

Kevin ran down the corridor. As he got closer to the door, he saw it was a truck loading dock, with an alley beyond. A short leap to the pavement, and he'd be free as a bird.

He sprinted out the door, to the edge of the dock. Tightening his grip on his ticket, he hurtled happily into the air.

For a moment he felt as if he were flying. But only a moment.

When he looked down, he saw the truth. He was falling into a trap. He pumped his arms and legs, desperately trying to change direction.

Below him, waiting with open arms, were Harry and Marv.

Chapter 14

"Gotcha!"

Harry caught Kevin in a crushing grip. Kevin struggled to get loose. Beside him, his airline ticket floated to the ground. He had to get it. It was his only way out.

His stomach sank as Marv bent over and snatched the ticket off the ground. "Hmm, look what I found," he said.

"Leave the trash alone, Marv," Harry said. "Give me a hand with this punk."

Marv stuffed the ticket into his pocket as Harry lowered Kevin to the ground. The two men grabbed him on either side and forced him out of the alley.

"You're in trouble, pal," Marv said.

"Look casual-like," Harry added. "Like we're taking a walk. If you try anything, you'll be sorry."

Marv chuckled. *"Real* sorry."

Kevin obeyed. They escorted him onto the crowded sidewalk, keeping a firm grip on his shoulders.

Harry's face was twisted into some kind of weird expression between rage and happiness. "We spent nine months in jail, thinking we had the worst luck in the universe," he said.

With his dangling right hand, Kevin groped for his Talkboy. He felt around the edge and secretly pressed RECORD. The machine came silently to life.

"We were wrong, little buddy," Harry went on.

"We're busted out of the clink and we're doing fine," Marv piped up like an excited kid. "And we're going to do even better. We ain't robbing houses no more. We're robbing *toy stores.* At midnight tonight, we're hitting Duncan's Toy Chest. Five floors of cash. Then we're going to get us phony passports — "

"You want to shut up, Marv?" Harry snapped.

"What's the difference?" Marv said. "He ain't going to talk to nobody — except maybe a fish. Or an undertaker."

"Let's just get him down to the subway tunnel. I'll feel a lot better when he's on ice."

Harry pulled the airline ticket out of his pocket. He held it up and read it. "One round trip to Miami, Florida. Get on the wrong plane, squirt?" With a grin, he tore the ticket in two. "You won't be needing this no more. American Airlines don't fly to the Promised Land, little dude."

He let the ticket pieces fall from his hand. As they floated to the sidewalk, Kevin's heart went along with them.

The three of them crossed Fifty-ninth Street, toward the park. Kevin's eyes went straight to a group of tourists on the opposite curb. They were standing around a mounted policeman, oohing and aahing about his horse.

Kevin tried desperately to think of a way to get the officer's attention.

"I got a gun in my pocket," Harry said out of the side of his mouth. "You open your mouth and you'll be able to spit your gum out through your forehead."

So much for that idea, Kevin thought. As Harry and Marv ducked their heads, Kevin cast a forlorn look at the officer.

The policeman smiled at Kevin and winked — a friendly kind of look any cop might give a kid. Then he turned away to talk to the tourists.

Harry sighed with relief. He yanked Kevin onto the curb and turned right. Together they waited for the green light with a lot of people on the corner of Fifth Avenue.

Kevin caught a whiff of exotic perfume. Directly in front of him was a gorgeous young woman. A model, he figured.

An idea flashed through his head. It was crazy. It was rude. He had no right to do it. But it might work.

He reached out and gave the woman a pinch.

She let out a shriek of surprise and wheeled around.

Marv blushed. He recognized her from the same corner, twenty-four hours ago — and from the toy store. Marv was glad she had no gorilla hand with which to hit him.

She used her right fist instead.

Marv spun away from the force of her blow. He let go of Kevin's hand.

Kevin turned on Harry. He uncorked a punch right into his stomach.

Harry dropped to his knees in pain. Kevin was free. He dashed to the stone wall and vaulted into Central Park.

His feet hit the ground running. He had no idea where he was going. He only wanted to put as much distance as possible between himself and those two goons.

How did they find him? What were they doing in New York? The questions flashed through Kevin's mind as he raced around a pond and up a hill.

He passed a zoo and a carousel. Then he passed the zoo again. The pathways were curving around, making him backtrack! He sprang to his left, but had to stop at a busy road. Taxis whizzed by in a yellow blur, for what seemed like hours. Finally he was able to cross. He ran down a wide path and ended up at a huge fountain overlooking a small lake. The plaza around the fountain was swarming with kids and their nannies. Kevin felt a little safer in the crowd.

Panting for breath, he sat on a stone bench. His eyes darted back in the direction he came from.

In the distance he could see Harry and Marv, running toward the fountain. Kevin got up and turned to run away.

Right by the edge of the plaza was a horse and buggy. The driver cheerfully pulled a blanket out of his rear compartment and handed it to a woman in the buggy. As he hopped into his seat and took the reins, he didn't notice Kevin watching him.

Moments later, Harry and Marv huffed and puffed into the plaza. Kevin was nowhere in sight. "Maybe we should take that," Marv said, pointing to the buggy.

But Harry wasn't listening. One by one, he yanked the hoods off the kids around him. The kids sneered and yelled at him, but Harry didn't care. Maybe one of them was Kevin. "We should have shot him when we had the chance," he said to Marv. "I hate pulling a job, knowing that kid's on the loose."

"What can he do?" Marv said with a shrug. "Kids are helpless."

"Not *that* kid!"

"He don't got a house full of dangerous goodies this time. He's alone. He's in the park. Grown-up men come in here and don't get out alive!"

Marv looked up at the sky. The sun was beginning to set. Soon the park would be dark. "Yeah," he said, his face lighting up with a devilish leer. "Good luck, little fella, wherever you are!"

Dragging their feet with fatigue, Harry and Marv shuffled out of the park. Maybe the kid was in worse danger without them.

A quarter of a mile north, the buggy turned into a narrow park road. The lid of its rear compartment slowly creaked open.

Kevin cautiously peered out. This wasn't exactly a comfortable hiding place. Not to mention the fact that it was getting awfully dark.

In the dimming sunlight, the trees looked gnarled and sinister. Their branches cast long, pointed shadows across the street. Around them, the park was clearing out fast. Joggers, parents with strollers, roller skaters — everyone seemed to be heading for the exits.

A wave of fear and loneliness shuddered through Kevin. He could feel his teeth chatter. For the first time since he'd been here, he was scared for his life.

"I want to go home," he whispered. A lonely, desperate question welled up from within. Casting his eyes up to the slate-gray sky, he let the words spill out.

"Mom, where are you?"

Chapter 15

Riiinnnng—

Kate McCallister snatched up the receiver before the phone finished its first ring. "Hello!" she said, her voice practically a shout. "Yes, this is she."

As she listened to the other end, her sleeping husband began to rouse from his contorted position on an armchair. The tinny sound of the television set drifted in from the adjoining room. There, all the McCallister kids were gathered on the bed and floor, watching the late late late movie.

"Oh, my God!" Mrs. McCallister exclaimed.

Her husband sat forward, his face both eager and wary. "What?"

Mrs. McCallister covered the mouthpiece and said, "It's the Miami police. They know where Kevin is!"

"Where?" Mr. McCallister asked.

She held up one finger and listened some more. "New York," she said to her husband. Then, into the phone: "I'm sure he was scared. He's not a troublemaker."

"What?" Mr. McCallister said.

She covered the mouthpiece again and said to her husband, "He used your credit card to check into the Plaza Hotel." Her voice rising with excitement, she spoke into the receiver. "Do they have him?"

Her face fell. "Uh-huh . . ."

"They don't have him?" Mr. McCallister asked.

His wife shook her head no. Mr. McCallister slammed his fist into the armchair in frustration.

"We'll catch the next flight," Mrs. McCallister said into the phone. "Thank you."

She hung up and slumped back on the bed. "He got away from the hotel people

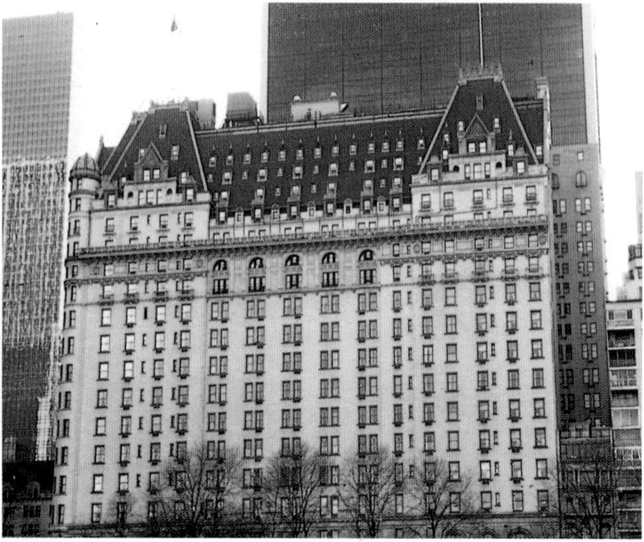

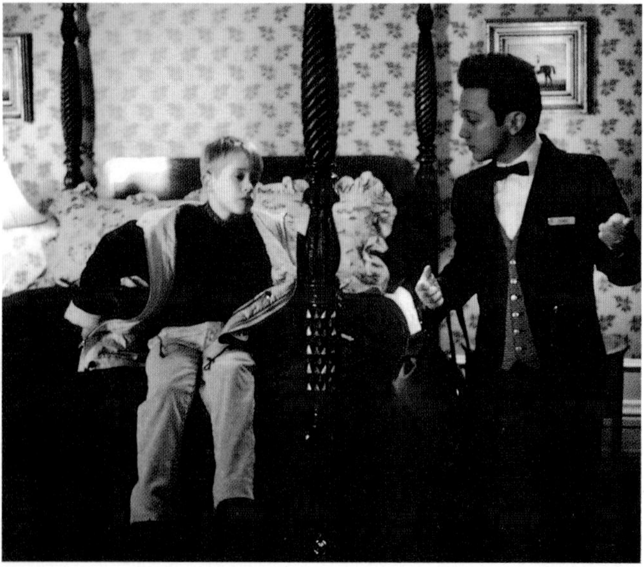

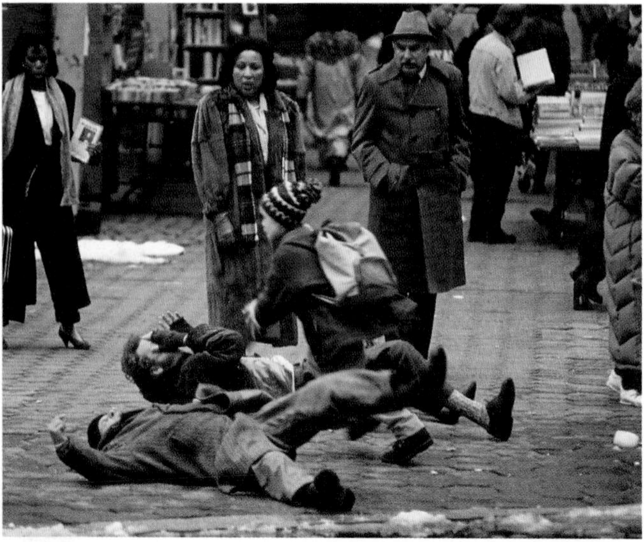

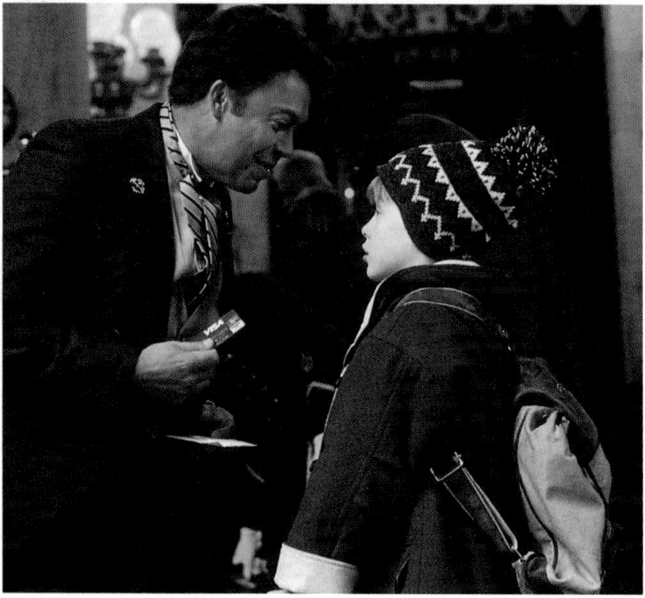
VISA

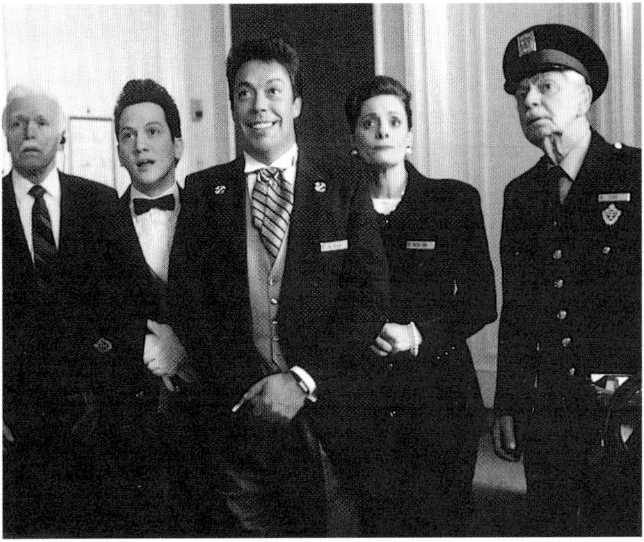

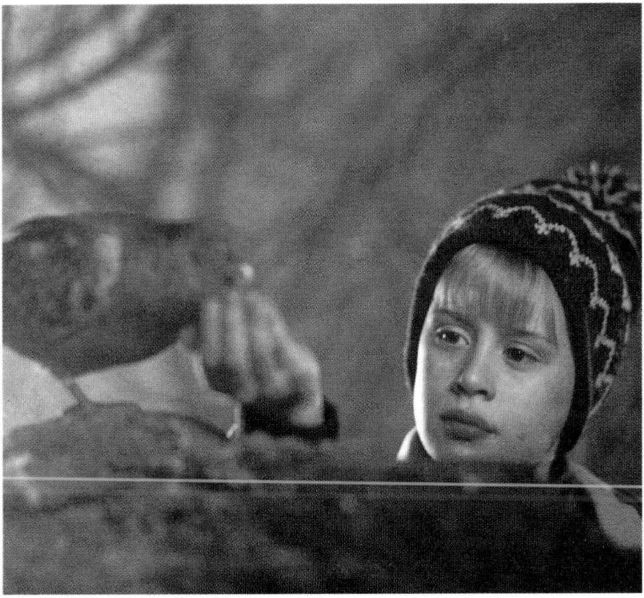

when they questioned him about the card. He must be scared."

"I wonder if he'd know enough to go to my brother's place?"

"They're in Paris."

"Maybe they have a house sitter."

"I thought they were renovating."

Mr. McCallister nodded. "You're right. They are, from top to bottom. The place is probably gutted."

They both fell into silence. Neither one wanted to voice their worst fears. Instead they just stared out the rain-soaked window as the television blared on.

A thousand miles to the north, Kevin looked across a wide street. He could see Central Park, dark and empty. But this was far from the Plaza and the noisy crowds of midtown. This neighborhood was quiet — *too* quiet. There were no stores, no nightlife. Just tall buildings, a little traffic, and the snow-dotted park.

Just looking at the park gave Kevin the creeps. It was a great place during the day, but he didn't want to go near it now. It seemed like hours ago that he'd been stuck in that buggy compartment. It was a good thing the buggy rode past an exit. He was able to hop out and make tracks to the sidewalk — alive.

Kevin looked up at a street sign: CENTRAL PARK WEST and 96TH STREET. Uncle Rob lived only a block away, on Ninety-fifth. Kevin went right, past a huge building that was under construction.

Uncle Rob's block was lined with spindly trees. Every square inch of curb space was taken up by parked cars. Occasional strings of Christmas lights could not make the dreary, old buildings look cheerful. They were almost all attached to one another. An alleyway ran next to a dark building, partially boarded up and covered with scaffolding.

Kevin walked past the boarded-up building and looked at its number: Fifty-one. Uncle Rob's address.

He went closer. There was definitely some major renovation work going on, although all the workers must have gone home. The scaffold was on the first floor, hanging from the roof by thick ropes. A metal chute slanted down from a third-floor window to a Dumpster on the street.

Some of the windows were covered with plywood. The ones that weren't were pitch-dark. A fire escape ran down the alley side of the building, where there was another Dumpster. In a sunken area under the stoop, there was a tiny garden, now filled with weeds and plaster chips.

Kevin walked up the stoop to a tall, carved-wood door. On it was a heavy, black-metal knocker. He pulled it back and let it thud against the door.

It echoed hollowly. Kevin waited, but no one answered.

Leaning over the stone banister, he peeked into a first-floor window. There was a stairway leading to the second floor. Next to it, Kevin could see a living room through an open set of tall wooden doors. Shelves lined the walls, covered with sheets of plastic. A ladder rested against a hole in the ceiling, and plaster and wires hung all over.

He pulled his head back. At about knee-level he noticed a hinged mail slot. Crouching, he pushed it open. He could see a foyer floor, which was actually made of loose plywood sheets. "Uncle Rob? . . . Anybody?" he called into the house.

No luck. He let the chute squeak shut.

Shoving his hands in his pockets, Kevin walked back down the steps. His breath made little white clouds in the frigid air. In a window across the street, he could see a family gathered around a Christmas tree, laughing and talking.

He looked away, trying to ignore the pain he felt inside. Where could he go now? Not the Plaza. If he showed his face there, he'd be arrested.

Kevin heard footsteps behind him. He turned to see a dark figure approaching. He didn't want to stick around and see who it was.

Picking up his pace, he walked to Central Park West and crossed to the other side of the street. The park's stone wall was the only familiar thing in this neighborhood. He turned right and followed the wall south. The midtown skyscrapers shone in the distance, probably miles away. Kevin decided to head in that direction. At least there would be more people around. Maybe he could duck into a theater or find a warm grating to sleep on.

A theater or a warm grating? In New York City? On Christmas Eve?

Kevin felt fear and sadness shooting through him. He wondered if he'd make it through the night. If the cold didn't finish him off, muggers would.

A woman walked toward Kevin from the other direction. She stared past him as if he weren't there. Clutching her coat against the wind, she looked as frightened as Kevin felt. He swerved to his left, walking nearer the park wall. A gust whistled through the trees, making the branches groan.

Kevin walked faster. His jaw was shivering, his eyes glued to the faraway lights of midtown.

And that was when his foot struck something solid. Kevin pitched forward.

"Watch it!" came an angry voice.

Kevin looked down. A man glared up at him from the sidewalk, his bloodshot eyes vivid against his soot-covered face. His body was wrapped in several layers of tattered clothing, and he mumbled curse words as he settled back into sleep.

Kevin recoiled in horror. That was

where the man was spending the night.

What am I so scared about? he thought.
I may be joining him!

He turned away. A man was coming his
way, clutching a bottle and staggering
from side to side. His eyes were half-shut,
and there were bits of icy foam on his
beard stubble.

Kevin broke into a run. He could feel
tears welling up, blurring his vision.
There were people all around him. Or
were they cars? Or trees? He moved his
legs as fast as they could go, but he felt
nothing. His body was numb.

Get a grip, he told himself. He blinked,
clearing his eyes. At the nearest corner,
a yellow cab waited at a stoplight.

Kevin ran into the street. "Hey!" he
screamed. "Taxi!"

He yanked open the rear door and
jumped in. Slamming the door behind
him, he sat back and exhaled. The air was
stale, but it felt warm.

"Boy, it's scary out there," Kevin said.

The cab driver turned around slowly.
Below his uneven crew cut, his face was
scarred and bruised. One of his eyes

seemed dead, and he looked like he hadn't shaved in weeks. He smiled at Kevin, revealing a mouth full of rotted teeth.

"Ain't much better in here," he growled.

Kevin screamed. He grabbed the door handle and pushed his way out of the cab.

There was no time to think. Kevin only knew one thing for sure — he had to get off the streets. There was no question. A kid couldn't be safe. If you weren't tripping over the living dead, you ended up in a car with a homicidal maniac.

He scuddered across the sidewalk, grabbed the top of the stone wall, and leapt into Central Park. His feet landed with a crunch in the crusty snow. A few yards ahead of him were a couple of huge boulders with a small space between them.

Kevin jammed himself into that space. He hoped no one had seen him. He hoped no one could hear the sledgehammer pounding of his heart.

He shifted his weight, trying to sit comfortably. The bags of Doritos crackled in his pocket. He pulled one out and ripped it open.

Hunger. He'd totally forgotten about it, but boy, was it there. Right alongside terror and fear.

"I don't want to ever take a vacation like this again," he said to himself as he shoved Doritos into his mouth.

Cooooooo . . . cooooooo . . .

Kevin stopped chewing. The Doritos remained an orange lump in his mouth. The sound was above him.

Slowly he looked up. A pigeon strutted on top of the rock, thrusting its head forward and backward.

Kevin smiled. He swallowed his Doritos, then pulled a small, broken piece out of the bag. Placing it in the middle of his palm, he held it out to the bird.

The pigeon cocked its head. It took a tentative couple of steps toward Kevin's hand, then snatched the Dorito in its beak.

"I guess you missed dinner, too," Kevin said. "My parents say I'm never supposed to touch birds, but you don't look so bad. You're a lot nicer than the people around here."

Kevin reached into his bag and broke off another piece of Dorito. But when he looked back, he saw that his little friend had company. There were now at least ten pigeons on the rock.

"Where did you guys come from?" Kevin asked.

Cooooooo . . . cooooooo . . . came his answer.

Kevin pulled another bag of Doritos out of his pocket. "I don't know if I have enough for everybody. How hungry are you guys?"

He opened the bag of Doritos, poured them into his hand, and crumbled them into pieces. But when he looked back up, the pigeons were facing the other way.

"What're you doing?" Kevin said, standing up. "Hey!"

One of the pigeons turned to face him. Kevin smiled. He began to hold out his hand.

The pigeon began to rise. Kevin stared at it. Its wings were not moving at all.

He realized there was something beneath the pigeon, pushing it upward. Hair. A forehead.

Slowly a familiar face appeared. The grizzled, grimy face of the pigeon lady.

She loomed higher as she climbed up

the other side. A few pigeons festooned her body, pecking at birdseed. Her eyes sized up Kevin, like the eyes of a witch preparing for a human sacrifice.

"AAAAAAAAAGGHHHHHHHH!"

Kevin didn't care who heard him. He didn't care if he woke the whole neighborhood. He didn't even care if a whole parkful of muggers came running. Right now the only thing on his mind was getting out.

He tried to lunge away from the rock, but he tripped and fell. He pulled on his right foot, but it wouldn't budge. He twisted it, pumped it.

Kevin felt the blood drain from his face. He was going nowhere. The foot was stuck, wedged between the rocks.

He felt a gust of hot breath as the pigeon lady knelt close to him. Closing his eyes, he braced himself for his last moments on Earth.

Chapter 16

Her bony fingers closed around his ankle. They gripped it tightly, sending an icy shiver through his leg.

She's going to twist it off, Kevin thought. Twist it off and drink the blood. Maybe feed him to the pigeons.

He sank to the ground, covering his face with his hands. Whatever she did, he didn't want to watch.

She squeezed. She twisted. She pushed down. She pulled up.

And then Kevin was free.

The pressure around his ankle was gone. He drew it nearer to him. Lowering his hands from his face, he turned around.

His ankle was still there, attached to his leg. He wiggled it, tucked it under himself.

The pigeon lady backed away, stepping down the other side of the rock. She had pulled him loose. That was all.

Her face disappeared from sight, taking the last of the pigeons. Kevin felt awful. She had helped him out, and all he had ever done for her was shriek and run away.

He stood up and walked around the boulder. The pigeon lady was shambling away from the rocks, the birds swaying to the rhythm of her body movement. Kevin went right up to her and smiled.

The pigeon lady's face fell. Her eyes hollowed with fright. She took a stuttering step backward.

"I'm sorry I screamed in your face," Kevin said. "You were just trying to help me . . . right?"

The pigeon lady's head bobbed in a grim, uncomfortable nod.

She's more afraid than I am, Kevin realized. He stepped forward, extending his hand. The pigeon lady backed away again. Her eyes darted from side to side, as if she were expecting an attack.

Kevin stayed put. "I'm Kevin McCallister," he said, trying to sound as friendly as he could.

The old woman stopped retreating.

"Your birds are real nice," Kevin went on.

This time there was a flicker of appreciation in her eyes. She nodded again, then reached into her coat. Taking out a handful of birdseed from some hidden pocket, she began feeding the flock of pigeons around her.

Kevin found a small ledge of rock and sat down to watch. This woman was quiet and weird, but somehow he felt more comfortable with her than with anyone else he'd met in New York. "I've seen you before," he said. "You had pigeons all over you. At first it looked kind of scary. But if you think about it, it's not so bad. They must be all over you because they like you."

The pigeon lady looked over her shoulder at Kevin. Their eyes met, then she turned back to her pigeons.

"If I'm bothering you, I can leave," Kevin volunteered. "Am I bothering you?"

The old woman's eyes suddenly softened. She opened her mouth to speak, but nothing came out. She shook her head, then tried again.

"No." Her voice was like an old, scratchy record. Kevin figured she hadn't spoken in a long, long time.

"Good," he said. "I'm not a pain in the behind?"

She shook her head again.

Kevin noticed that the trees above were crowded with pigeons. He looked up and asked, "Will those pigeons come back on their own or do you have to call them?"

Silently the pigeon lady reached into her coat pocket and took out a fistful of seed. With her other hand, she opened Kevin's palm. Then she poured the seed into his hand and made an underhand tossing motion.

Kevin threw the seed on the ground.

"They can hear it," the woman whispered.

In a sudden, swooping motion that filled the sky, the pigeons flew down to the seed.

As they began pecking away, Kevin grinned. "That's great!"

He watched them for a moment, until he felt himself shivering. Maybe the pigeons didn't mind the weather, but he sure did.

"It's pretty cold out," Kevin said. "I could sure go for a cup of hot chocolate. How about you?"

The pigeon lady said nothing. Her face tightened a bit, as if she weren't sure about trusting Kevin.

"Coffee?" Kevin suggested. "My treat."

With a slight nod, the pigeon lady began walking to the park exit. Kevin walked beside her, looking around at the park. Empty park benches lined the walkways, which were lit by pools of light from the old-fashioned street lamps.

The woman led Kevin back into the Ninety-sixth Street subway station, where they took a train to midtown. She seemed to know exactly where to go, but she wouldn't tell Kevin.

They came up into a well-lit street, crammed with Christmas Eve shoppers and tourists. Jingling bells mixed with car horns and the underground rumbling of the subway. At a nearby coffee shop, Kevin bought coffee and hot chocolate.

He carried the two cardboard cups out to the sidewalk. "Now where?" he asked.

"Come," was all the woman said.

He walked with her to the next corner. Kevin stared at a bright marquee across the intersection. It was an entire block long, with an entranceway decorated in shining gold. Parents and kids rushed in through the door, all dressed up and beaming with excitement. Above them, enormous neon letters spelled out RADIO CITY MUSIC HALL.

"Wow . . ." Kevin said.

The pigeon lady just trundled onward, leading Kevin around the entrance. On the side of the theater were a few unmarked doors without knobs. One of them was propped open with a trash can.

The old woman signaled Kevin to wait, then walked slowly past the door. She peered inside, then waved Kevin toward her.

Together they walked through the door and into a dim corridor. There was an old metal staircase to the right. Directly ahead, the corridor turned sharply left.

Around the corner, Kevin could hear voices. The old woman ignored them, leading him up the stairs with surprising quickness.

They climbed and climbed, spiraling around, until they reached an old, unmarked trapdoor. The pigeon lady pushed upward.

Creeeeeak! It opened onto a narrow, flat section of roof. A few feet in front of them was a wall with high-arching windows caked with years of grime. A pane in one of the windows was missing, and the window itself was ajar. The old woman stepped through the opening. Kevin followed her into an indoor cavern, an enormous room with high ceilings and electronic equipment on the walls. Clusters of huge theatrical lamps were scattered around the floor, shining intense beams of colored light downward through metal grates. Kevin could hear orchestra music coming from below them.

His eyes widened. "Are we . . . above the stage?"

The pigeon lady nodded. She walked across the room, carefully making her way around wires and electronic equipment. Kevin heard a fluttering noise behind them. He looked around to see a pigeon flying in through the missing windowpane. It flew up to join a group of pigeons on rafters above them.

Next to a wide floor grating, the pigeon lady sat down. Kevin joined her, handing her the coffee. She gestured toward the grating, and Kevin looked through.

The brightness blinded him for a moment. But as his eyes cleared, he could see a polished wooden stage that looked as big as a football field. Kids danced around a Christmas tree, next to taller dancers dressed up as toys. An orchestra played loudly, sitting between the stage and an audience that was jammed with people.

"The Nutcracker Suite!" Kevin said. "I've seen it — but not like this!"

For the first time, the corners of her mouth began to rise. Kevin knew she wanted to smile, but her mouth muscles probably hadn't moved that way in a while.

"Nice music," he said.

The pigeon lady nodded. "And it's warm."

"Do you live here?" Kevin asked.

"Here? No, I have an apartment."

Good. She was loosening up a little, beginning to sound like a normal person. Kevin wanted to know all about her. "Do you have kids?"

The old woman's eyes misted over. "No. I wanted them, but the man I loved fell out of love with me. It broke my heart. And then every time a chance to be loved came by, I ran from it. You might say I stopped trusting people."

"No offense," Kevin said, "but that seems sort of a dumb thing to do."

"I was afraid," the woman replied with a sigh, "afraid of getting my heart broken again. You know, sometimes you can trust a person, and when things are down, they forget about you."

Kevin knew what she meant. He'd been forgotten about, too. But still, even after last year and this, he knew his family loved him. "Maybe they're just too busy," he said with a shrug. "Maybe they don't forget you, they just . . . forget to remember you. I don't think people mean to forget."

147

"I'm just afraid if I trust anyone, I'll get my heart broken again."

"I understand *that*. I used to have this really nice pair of roller skates, and I was afraid that if I wore them I'd wreck them. So I kept them in the box. And you know what happened?"

"What?"

"I outgrew them. I never used them once outside. I just wore them in my room a couple of times."

The pigeon lady chuckled. "A person's heart and their feelings are a little different than skates."

"It's kind of the same thing," Kevin said. "If you aren't going to use your heart, what's the difference if it gets broken? If you keep it to yourself, maybe it'll be like my roller skates. When you do decide to try it, it won't be any good. You should take a chance. You've got nothing to lose."

The old lady's brow creased. She looked deep in thought. "There's some truth there."

"I think so. Your heart might still be broken, but it's not gone. If it was gone, you wouldn't be this nice."

"You know," the pigeon lady said, sighing, "it's been a couple of years since I even talked to someone."

Kevin shrugged. "That's okay, you're really good at it. You're not boring, you don't mumble or spit when you talk. You should do it more often. I think you'd just have to wear an outfit that doesn't have pigeon poop on it."

With a real smile, the pigeon lady said, "I was working pretty hard at keeping people away."

"I always think I'll have a lot of fun if I'm alone. But then, when I *am* alone, it isn't fun at all. I don't care how much some people bug me sometimes, I'd rather be with somebody than by myself."

"So what are you doing running around the streets on Christmas Eve? Did you get in trouble?"

Kevin lowered his head. "Yeah."

"You did something wrong, didn't you?" the woman said knowingly.

"A lot of things."

"A good deed erases a bad deed. You know that."

"Well, it's pretty late. I don't know if I'm going to have enough time to do all the good deeds I need to erase all the bad ones I did."

"You'll be fine," the pigeon lady reassured him. "It's Christmas Eve. Good deeds count extra tonight."

"They do?"

"That's right. You think of the most important thing you can do for others right now, and then you go do it."

Kevin thought about that. He wasn't sure what that "important thing" would be. But in the remaining hours before Christmas, he'd find *something* to erase his bad deed. "Okay," he said.

Kevin stood up, ready to get started. He looked the pigeon lady straight in the eye. "If I don't see you again, I hope everything turns out okay."

"Thanks," she replied.

"Say good-bye to your birds for me."

"I will."

Kevin began walking to the open window. He would miss the old woman. In a funny way, they had some things in common. The main difference was, Kevin had not lost hope. At least, not yet.

At the window, he turned back around.

"If you need somebody to trust, it can be me. I won't forget to remember you."

"Don't make any promises you can't keep," the pigeon lady said softly.

"Merry Christmas," Kevin said, stepping through the window.

"Merry Christmas."

Kevin ducked back onto the roof. The last thing he saw before climbing through the trapdoor was the pigeon lady's warm smile as she waved good-bye.

Chapter 17

Clank!

The empty soda can fell into the metal trash basket and bounced around. Kevin stared at it for a moment. He had just cleaned the New York City sidewalks of one piece of litter. Definitely a good deed.

But not much of one. Cans and papers and cigarette butts were all over the place. Good deeds might count extra tonight, but one little can was probably the lowest on the point scale.

"That won't do it," he said aloud. "I'd have to wash the whole city."

Kevin sat down on the curb to think. He wondered where he was. He'd been walking quite a while, and the neighborhood was much quieter than midtown. There were no office buildings, just low-rise apartment houses like the ones on his uncle's block.

He thought about the kids inside the apartments. How many of them were going to wait up for Santa tonight? How many were going to get the presents they always wanted? Kevin imagined being a lucky New York kid, waking up to a train set like the one at Duncan's Toy Chest.

The thought of the toy store gave Kevin a sudden chill. Right now, Harry and Marv were probably getting ready to rob the place. He imagined the look on poor old Mr. Duncan's face when he discovered all his cash registers empty.

Kevin's eyes focused on a bright light at the end of the block. It was a huge, five-pointed star, shining over the roofs of the buildings across from Kevin. Kevin figured it was on top of a taller building, one block to his left.

He remembered seeing this star once before, outside his window at the Plaza. Back then, he was looking down on the star, feeling on top of the world. Now?

Well, now the star seemed so high and so powerful. And it seemed to be beckoning Kevin toward it.

He stood up and walked to the end of the block. At the intersection, the building beneath the star came into full view.

Above the main entrance was a sign, illuminated by plain yellow lights:

NEW YORK CHILDREN'S HOSPITAL

Kevin knew about this place — this was where Mr. Duncan was going to take all the Christmas Eve earnings from his store.

Or so the old man thought. He'd be lucky if Harry and Marv left a dime.

Kevin's mind began to race. There had to be a way to stop them. Calling the police? That was risky. They wouldn't believe a kid. Besides, after what happened at the Plaza, there was probably an arrest warrant out for him. For all he knew, his photo might be on post office bulletin boards tomorrow.

Who else could he call? If only Uncle Rob were in town. He was a New Yorker. He could help Kevin.

Suddenly an idea started to form. His eyes drifted upward to the star. He could feel its warmth, even down at the sidewalk. Its light seemed to seep into him, clearing his thoughts.

There *was* a way to get those two slime balls. It was a long shot, but it was better than not trying.

Kevin smiled. "Thanks," he said to the star.

At the sound of footsteps, he lowered his eyes. A couple was coming through the main entrance of the hospital. They passed between two lit-up Christmas trees on either side of the entrance. Bundling against the cold, they walked away down the street.

Then a little circle began to form in the wintery frost of a first-floor window. Through the circle, a small face looked out. It was a boy, dressed in his pajamas. His sad, misty eyes followed the couple until they were out of sight.

Kevin felt a lump in his throat. Poor little guy, he thought. No wonder Mr. Duncan liked to go to the hospital on Christmas. When you thought about it, Harry and Marv weren't stealing from

Duncan's Toy Chest. They were stealing from that kid.

And that made Kevin mad. "You can mess with a lot of things," he said under his breath, "but you can't mess with kids at Christmas!"

It was time to put his plan into action. He remembered that Central Park was at the end of the next block. If he followed the park wall uptown, he knew he'd get to his uncle's house. That was where his plan was going to start.

His feet flew. Rounding the corner of Central Park West, he sprinted uptown. To his right, the hills of the park seemed to rise and fall as he ran.

BONNNNG! BONNNNG! BONNNNG!

From a nearby church came the chiming of bells. Solemn, deep chimes.

Kevin felt a lonely sadness tugging at him from inside, but he kept it in.

If this crazy plan worked, it *would* be a merry Christmas.

The street signs whizzed by. By the time he reached Ninety-fifth Street, his leg muscles were screaming with pain. But there was no time to think about that.

He had to get inside his uncle's house, somehow.

The door was out of the question. It was locked and about a foot thick. All the windows were boarded up or closed, too.

Except for one.

Kevin's eyes followed the rubbish chute from the Dumpster all the way up to the third floor. It was made of short metallic segments, so there were probably handholds — and the only way rubbish could come down was through an open window!

Kevin hoisted himself onto the edge of the Dumpster, then crawled into the chute. Gripping the joints between the segments, he scampered upward.

It was dusty, cold, and pitch-black. It groaned beneath Kevin's weight. But it held up — and there *was* an open window at the top.

Kevin tumbled into a room on the third floor. A street lamp shone through another window, giving the room a dull, amber glow. In the corner, bedroom furniture was huddled together under drop cloths. Next to it was a large metal tool chest and some paint supplies.

The idea was taking shape in his head. It was complex, much more so than anything Kevin had ever dreamed up before. It would help to write it all down. Kevin grabbed a marker off the floor.

OPERATION HO HO HO, he scribbled on the wall. The perfect name. Writing furiously in the street-lamp light, he mapped out a battle plan. He committed it to memory and sprang into action.

Step One began at the tool chest. He yanked it open and looked inside.

His eyes lit up. It had everything he needed. He quickly pulled out a wood saw, a metal saw, a hammer, a rope, an electric drill, some cheesecloth, a pair of leather work gloves, and a screwdriver. At the bottom he found a butane torch and flare.

He took them out, too. They'd come in handy.

Step Two. Begin at the basement and work up. With the screwdriver, the torch, and the cheesecloth in his pocket, Kevin sped down the stairs to the second floor. There was a door at the bottom of the stairs with no knob. Kevin pushed it open into a room crammed with metal pipes, wood planks, cans of paint, buckets of plaster, and another saw — all stuff he could use. He noticed part of the floor was missing, and a ladder led down to the first-floor living room.

He clambered down, jumped to the floor, and ran straight to the front foyer. The foyer's floor was made of loose plywood slats, just as he'd seen through the mail slot earlier. Carefully he slid one of the slats away. It was resting on some wooden beams. Between the beams, Kevin could see straight through to the basement.

He lowered himself on one of the beams and dropped into the basement. It was partially aboveground; light came in through the tops of windows. There was a door in the back, which led to a small yard. Shelves lined the walls, crammed with more stuff: paint cans, ropes, rolls of silver electrical tape, a hot-glue gun, and a staple gun.

Kevin went to work. He pulled out his plastic Monster Sap bottle and began squeezing the slippery goo all over the floor. Then he pried open each can of paint with the screwdriver, and left them on the shelves.

Next he filled the cheesecloth with glue from the hot-glue gun and put it on a shelf. That was the last part. Grabbing a can of kerosene, some rope, electrical tape, and the staple gun, he went up the stairs.

Step Three. The first floor. He ran to the kitchen, where there was a plumber's bag and lots of loose wrenches. Just outside the kitchen was a back door. Over it Kevin hung the plumber's bag from the ceiling. He tied another rope from the doorknob to the bag's zipper. Then he loosened the knob with his screwdriver. On his way out, he grabbed a box of matches and stuffed them into his pocket.

Next stop, the bathroom. He dumped the kerosene into the toilet, then hung the torch on a hook. With a cord, he tied the torch's trigger to the bathroom light switch.

He ran to the front door, taking care to step around the missing floor. Using the screwdriver, he removed the screws from the doorknob. He pulled out the inside half, leaving the outer one intact. Now only a thin piece of metal jutted through the knob hole toward Kevin. He tied a rope around it, attaching the other end to the staple-gun handle. Then he taped the staple gun tightly to the door. The staple ejector hung into the doorknob hole. One pull from the outside, and whammo!

Giggling, Kevin then dragged a heavy bag of plaster to the edge of the foyer. Tying another cord around the bag, he let the rope dangle through the floor and into the basement.

Kevin raced through the final steps.

Four. The scaffold. He put open cans of varnish on one end of it, opposite the pile of bricks.

Five. The second floor. First he sawed halfway through the top rung of the ladder. Then he tied a rope around a metal pipe and placed it at the top of the stairs that led down. Next to the pipe he placed a few empty paint cans.

Six. The third floor. He tied a rope to the tool chest and tossed *that* rope down the stairs.

Seven. The roof. There, under the dark winter sky, he tied a thick coil of rope to a hundred-pound bag of cement by the roof's edge. He coiled the rest of the rope into a can of kerosene. Then he gathered some bricks into a neat pile, and left the leather work gloves in plain sight.

And finally, *Eight*. The fire escape. Kevin ran downstairs and outside. With a paint roller and a long extension, he stood on his toes and smeared Monster Sap all over the fire escape.

Done! The booby trap was set. Operation Ho Ho Ho was in place and ready for implementation.

Now for the implementees.

Grabbing a long wooden plank and a can of paint, Kevin ran out to Central Park West. A yellow cab whizzed by, heading south. "Taxi!" he called out.

SCREEEEEEEEEECH!

The brakes squealed as the driver stopped the car. Kevin leaned into the passenger window for a look at the driver's face.

He looked human. A good sign.

Kevin jumped in the back of the cab. "Duncan's Toy Chest, and make it fast!" he commanded.

As the cab took off, Kevin settled back in his seat.

The fun part was about to begin.

Chapter 18

"What kind of hotel lets a child check in alone?"

Kate McCallister's voice resounded through the lobby of the Plaza Hotel. She was furious. No, furious was too mild a word. Insane with anger. Ready to kill. *That* was how she felt.

It didn't matter that American Airlines had given her whole family free tickets to New York. It didn't matter that a police escort had been waiting at the airport to take them to the Plaza. It didn't even matter that the Plaza had agreed to put them up for free overnight.

She could *never* forgive what they had done.

Behind the check-in desk, the clerk tried to smile. "The boy had a convincing story," she explained. "He had a credit card, a reservation — "

"What kind of idiots do you have working for you?" Mrs. McCallister screamed.

"The finest in New York, ma'am," the clerk stammered.

Mrs. McCallister could barely speak. Her jaws were locked together. It took all she had to stop herself from lunging across the desk.

"It's Christmas Eve," she said, her voice a poisonous growl, "and because of you, *my son is lost in one of the biggest cities in the world!*"

In the cab, Kevin pulled out the Plaza stationery from his pack and began scribbling a letter. When he finished, he stuffed the letter in the envelope and wrote on it, *To Mr. Duncan (The Guy Who Owns the Store).* He would use this in the next part of his plan. As the cab rounded the south side of the park, Kevin wrapped a rubber band around his letter and put it in his pocket.

Kevin made the cabdriver stop a block from Duncan's Toy Chest. If Harry and Marv saw a cab stopping in front, Operation Ho Ho Ho was sure to become Operation Uh-Oh.

He got out, taking the plank and the paint can, and walked the rest of the way. In front of Duncan's, he crouched low. He could see movement inside. Putting his equipment next to the wall, he peered through the window.

There they were, at the top of the escalator. It had been turned off for the night, so Harry and Marv were able to walk slowly down, looking left and right. As they got to the bottom, they pulled crowbars out of their coats. With a grin, Harry turned to Marv.

Kevin strained to hear what they were saying.

"Bars up," came Harry's voice faintly through the window.

"Bars up," Marv replied.

They clinked crowbars together and went to the cash register. With a sharp jab, each of them wedged his bar under the cash drawer and forced it open.

Kevin had to work fast. He set the can directly under the window, then tried to balance the plank evenly on it. Next he took out the letter he'd written in the cab. He needed one more thing — a big rock. He looked around frantically. Where would he find a rock on a city street?

Inside, Harry and Marv were in Crook Heaven. They pried open register after register, stuffing wads of cash into a gym bag.

Marv was beaming. "There's more money in this place than I ever dreamed!" he said.

"It makes you wonder why we spent so much time robbing private homes," Harry replied, gleefully snatching a fistful of money.

"The amazing thing is," Marv said, "we're fugitives from the law, we're up to our elbows in cash money — and there isn't anybody who knows about it!"

As they jabbered and stuffed, Kevin ran to a construction site around the corner. There he found a huge, dirt-covered stone, which had been dug up from the street. He took out the note he had written in the cab, wrapped it around the stone with the rubber band, and ran back to the store.

Kevin planted himself outside the front window. He pulled his Polaroid camera from his backpack and set it within reach. He clasped the rock firmly. His breaths came quick and shallow. Inside, Harry and Marv were finishing up.

He looked at his hand. Between his fingers he could read *To Mr. Duncan* in his own handwriting.

His last bit of hesitation melted away. He owed this to the old man.

"This is it," Kevin said softly, setting the rock next to the camera. "There's no turning back. Another Christmas in the trenches."

Knock-knock-knock!

Kevin rapped sharply on the window. The sound echoed in the store.

Harry and Marv froze. Dollar bills hung out of their fists like lettuce from the sides of a sandwich. They stared at Kevin, their mouths hanging open.

"He's back," Marv said in disbelief.

Kevin grabbed his camera and held it to his eye.

Click! The flash bathed Harry and Marv in a ghostly white light. A picture zipped out the front of the camera.

Harry's eyes were as wide as baseballs. "He took our picture!"

"How does my hair look?" Marv asked.

Kevin stuffed the camera and the photo into his backpack. He grabbed the stone and reared back.

The windup . . . the pitch . . .

Harry opened his mouth to yell.

CRRRAAAAAAASHHHHH!

The rock hurtled through the window. Shards of glass rained into the store. With an earsplitting shriek, a burglar alarm pierced the air.

Harry and Marv leapt over the cashier counter. They headed for the nearest exit — the broken window.

Harry came sailing out first. He landed on the end of the wooden plank. It crashed against the sidewalk, like one end of a seesaw.

A knowing smirk grew across his face.

"Nice try, kid," he said to Kevin. "I ain't that stupid."

Next came Marv. He landed feetfirst — at the other end of the seesaw.

"Who-o-o-o-o-o-oa!" Harry vaulted straight up into the air.

"Harry?" Marv called out, looking up.

Windmilling his arms, Harry came crashing to the pavement. Marv scrambled to help him up.

Kevin ran across the street. He spun around and aimed his camera at the two crooks.

Click!

Harry turned in the direction of the flash. "There he is!"

Kevin took off. Around him the quiet streets had burst into life. Police sirens wailed in the distance. Harry and Marv's frantic footsteps whapped against the pavement behind him.

He ran up a side street, heading straight for Central Park. His uncle's house was on the other side. If he could get through alive — and not lose the two goons . . .

He leapt over the wall. Harry and Marv

followed behind. Kevin went right, cutting across fields and horse paths.

It seemed like years before he got to his uncle's house. But as he rounded Ninety-fifth Street, Harry and Marv were right behind him.

Kevin jumped on top of the Dumpster. He crawled into the chute and began climbing. At the top, he hopped through the window and went straight for the stairway to the roof.

He burst out the roof door and ran to the edge. The bricks, the kerosene bucket with the rope inside, the bag of cement — everything was in place.

Kevin looked down. Harry and Marv were standing in front of the house, looking around. Harry was still holding tightly onto his gym bag.

Kevin had them right where he wanted them. He pulled out his camera again. Cupping his hands to his mouth, he yelled, "I'm up here! Come and get me!"

Operation Ho Ho Ho had officially begun.

Chapter 19

Harry and Marv looked up.

Click! Kevin took another photo.

Gritting his teeth with fury, Harry pulled his crowbar out of his coat. "Bars up!" he growled.

Marv took his out, too. "Bars up!" He clanked it against Harry's. "Let's *kill*."

Marv stepped toward the front stoop, but Harry pulled him back. "Hold on, pea brain," Harry said. "We got busted last time because we underestimated that little bundle of misery. We don't go after him until *we've* got a plan that we're sure is better than *his* plan."

"This ain't like last time, Harry," Marv

said. "This ain't his house. He's running scared. He ain't got a plan."

Harry raised a scornful eyebrow. "May *I* do the thinking, please?"

Putting on as sweet a smile as he could, Harry looked up at Kevin. "Sonny?"

Kevin peeked over.

"Nothing would thrill me more greatly than to shoot you," Harry continued. "Knocking off a youngster ain't going to mean all that much to me. You understand?"

Kevin just stared blankly.

"But since I'm in a hurry," Harry went on, "I'm going to make you a deal. You throw down your camera and we won't hurt you. You won't never see us again. Okay? Sound good?"

"Promise?" Kevin called down.

"Cross my heart," Harry replied.

Kevin took the camera from around his neck. "Okay!"

In one quick movement, he set the camera down and picked up a brick.

Harry squinted. He couldn't see exactly what Kevin was doing. He put his gym bag down near the building's sunken garden, then held out his arms. "Give it to me, kid!"

That was just what Kevin did. He dropped the brick over the side.

Harry smiled. Beside him, Marv happily picked at his teeth.

BONK! The brick bounced off Marv's head. Marv slumped to the sidewalk.

"Direct hit!" Kevin said to himself.

Marv sat up, rubbing his head. Harry knelt next to him, holding up three fingers. "How many fingers am I holding up?" he asked.

"Eight," Marv said, squinting.

Harry snarled with anger. "You want to throw bricks?" he yelled up to Kevin. "Go ahead, throw another one!"

He asked for it, Kevin thought. He let another one fly over the rooftop, right at Harry.

In the nick of time, Harry ducked away.

BONK! Marv got it again.

Harry grinned in triumph. "If you can't do no better than that kid, you're going to lose!"

Marv lifted his head. His eyes were full

of panic. "Harry," he pleaded. "No."

Kevin let loose another one. Harry ducked again.

BONK! Marv collapsed to the ground, unconscious.

"Got any more?" Harry shouted up to Kevin.

He waited and watched, but Kevin's head stayed behind the roof's half-wall. That was it, Harry thought. There were no more bricks. The dumb kid wasn't *that* hard to outsmart.

He knelt next to his partner. "Come on, Marv, get up."

Marv's eyes fluttered open and shut. He tried to focus on Harry.

Then he looked over Harry's shoulder, and his eyes snapped open. "Harry!" he screamed, pointing to the sky.

Harry turned just in time. A brick was heading right toward him. He sprang out of the way.

BONK!

Marv was getting use to it. He barely even felt that one. In fact, he kind of enjoyed it. He could hear twittering birds and see sensational colors.

"That kid's dead," Harry declared. "Nobody throws bricks at me and gets away with it."

Harry stormed into the alley. He would try to climb the fire escape.

Inside, Kevin raced down the stairs.

Marv waited for the birds and colors to fade. Then he got up and marched straight for the front door. He had a job to do.

He went up the front steps and clasped the doorknob. He turned it and pulled.

It came off in his hand, attached to a thin piece of rope. Marv looked at the rope, befuddled. It led into the house, through the doorknob hole. He pulled, and more of the rope came out. He pulled again and again.

Finally the rope went taut. He gave it a hard yank. Nothing happened.

Marv was determined to open the door. Maybe if he pulled hard enough . . .

He wrapped the entire rope tightly around his hand. Then he stepped over it, turning his back to the door. This would be a better angle. He could really put his strength into it.

His behind was against the doorknob hole as he pulled with all his might.

Ca-chunk!

Marv's eyes bulged. All the pain in his head was forgotten. Now there was a new pain. Sharp. Sudden. And excruciating.

His mouth dropped open in silent agony. He was beyond screaming.

The string was stapled to him, right above his rear pocket. Gingerly he lifted his leg over the string. Slowly the string pulled again.

Ca-chunk!

This time he got it in the front. He saw black. He doubled over at the waist. His head pitched forward . . .

Ca-chunk!

"Ouch!"

Marv straightened up. He grabbed his hat and tried to pull it off.

No luck. It stayed put.

He pulled again, harder.

Pinnnng! The staple flew out and landed on the ground. The hat came loose.

"Yiiiiiiiii!" Marv hopped around in pain. When he stopped, he realized the rope had snapped. He was free. No more staples.

Marv's eyes were on fire. He had had enough. "I'm coming in!" he shouted.

He charged the door with his shoulder. The door burst open. Marv flew into the foyer. He braced himself for a fall.

But he wasn't prepared for the fall Kevin had planned! Screaming, Marv plunged through the missing floor and thudded onto the cement below.

In the alley outside, Harry hoisted himself onto the Dumpster. He balanced himself carefully on the edge. The fire escape was a short jump upward. If he did it just right, he could climb to the roof.

He bent his knees and sprang. It was a powerful jump. He knew he'd make it. His hands clasped a bar at the bottom of the fire escape. His body swung forward.

Then . . . *shhloop*. Harry's fingers slid off the Monster Sap. He flew forward and landed with a thud in the alley.

"You stinking little . . ." Harry was furious. He picked himself up and staggered around to the back. There was a porch there, with a back door.

He grabbed the doorknob. It spun loosely in his hand. Harry smiled. "You're going to have to do better than this, kid!" he shouted.

Rearing back with his leg, he gave a sharp kick. The door crashed open.

Harry rushed inside. Above him, Kevin's rope pulled open the zipper of the plumber's bag. Metal wrenches showered out.

Each of them landed squarely on Harry's head.

"Yeeeeeoow!" Harry fell to the floor. Grimacing in agony, he struggled to his feet. This wasn't going to stop him. Nothing would. He had this kid's number now. He would look for traps in each room.

He stumbled through a dark, narrow pantry and flicked on a light switch. No tricks here. No kid either.

Next was a hallway. Cautiously he pulled a string overhead. A light plinked on. He looked around, but there were no surprises here, either.

Just off the hall was a bathroom. He decided to peek inside there. He stepped in and flicked the switch.

He didn't see that there was a rope attached to the switch. And he didn't see it pull the trigger of the blowtorch on the wall.

But he felt the result.

With a roar of flame, the torch blasted the back of Harry's head.

"AAAAAAAAAGGGHHHHH!" In the bathroom mirror, Harry saw the back of his head engulfed in fire. He twisted the sink water faucets.

No water.

He tried to pat the fire out with his hands, but it was too hot. Then he saw the toilet. It was filled with nice, cool, clear water.

Harry dunked his head in.

BOOOOOOOOOOM!! It may have looked like water, but it exploded like kerosene.

Harry stood up slowly, his face blackened, his collar charred. This was it. This was the last straw.

Chapter 20

In the basement, Marv shook himself into consciousness. Every muscle in his body ached — not to mention the staple cuts. That kid was asking for it. When Marv found him, there would be no mercy.

He stood up and took a step forward.

Right into the Monster Sap.

"Who-o-o-o-o-oa!" Marv's legs went out from under him. He landed on the floor with a *thunk*.

Ha! The old slime trick, he thought. Well, if you just braced yourself carefully and slid, like an ice skater . . .

He got up and steadied himself. Then

he slid his leg forward. He glided across the floor. It was working!

Well, almost. He hadn't thought about stopping.

He slipped closer to the shelving unit on the opposite wall. The shelving unit with the open paint cans.

CRRRRRASSSH!

The shelves came down. Paint glopped over Marv's hair. It coated his face and splashed onto his clothes.

"Auuugh!" The worst part was the stinging in his eyes. Standing up, he tried to wipe them off, but his hands and sleeves were both drenched.

He could squint enough to see a small piece of cheesecloth on the floor. That would work. He picked it up and tried to wipe his eyes.

But the cheesecloth wasn't really *wiping*. In fact, it was stuck to his skin! He gave it a desperate pull.

Rrrrrrip!

"Yeeeeeow!"

Reeling with pain, Marv looked down at the cloth. His eyebrows, mustache, and goatee were there — completely removed by the glue from Kevin's hot-glue gun.

Marv threw the cloth down. There had to be another way out. A way that didn't involve much walking.

Over his shoulder, he spotted a dangling rope. It led back up into the foyer. He reached up and gave it a tug. It held fast.

He tugged harder. It seemed strong enough to hold him.

Marv began hoisting himself upward. His legs left the floor.

Just outside the foyer, the force of Marv's weight pulled the bag of plaster closer to the missing floor . . . and closer . . .

When Marv noticed the burlap sliding over the hole above him, he tried to scramble down.

Too late. The bag fell over the side. It smacked Marv on the head, sending him back to the basement.

He hit bottom in a cloud of thick, white dust. Coughing and spitting, he pushed himself to his feet. "I'm going to murder that kid!" he vowed.

Taking care to step on the plaster, not the Sap, Marv retrieved the rope. He tossed it over one of the foyer's exposed floor beams. *That* was strong enough to hold his weight.

His eyes stinging with anger — not to mention paint and plaster — he raised himself toward the first floor.

Kevin was waiting upstairs in the living room. He stood next to the open double doors. He could hear Marv grunting in the foyer and Harry mumbling in the bathroom. Now was the time for the next phase.

"Don't you guys know that a kid always wins against two idiots?" he taunted.

In the bathroom, Harry stopped wiping the soot off his face. He turned toward the sound of the voice.

Kevin turned and ran toward the ladder — just as Marv peeked up over the foyer floor. "Harry!" he shouted. "He's in the living room!"

Harry clomped out of the bathroom. He got to the living room in time to see Kevin disappearing up the ladder and through the hole to the second floor. Grabbing the rickety ladder, he began climbing himself.

When he got near the top, he felt the ladder sag. He looked up. The top rung, which had been cut halfway through, was breaking under Harry's weight.

With a snap, it gave way. Harry plummeted to the floor.

As he landed with a loud crash, Marv skidded into the room. He looked at Harry, then looked up. "He went upstairs."

"No kidding!" Harry snapped. "Come on, help me up!"

As Marv gave his partner a hand, Kevin's head appeared in the hole in the ceiling. "Why don't you guys try the stairs?" he suggested.

The two of them rushed to the bottom of the stairs. But just as they started to climb, Harry pulled Marv back. "Hold on," he said.

Harry stomped on the first step, running in place, then quickly stepped down and backed away.

An empty paint can came sailing down the stairs. It landed harmlessly on the floor.

Harry gave Marv a knowing grin. "Owwww!" Harry yelled.

Marv giggled at the trick.

"That's one," Harry whispered.

Marv nodded. "I'll get him, Harry!" he yelled loudly. He jumped on the first step and repeated what Harry had done.

Another paint can flew downward. Marv ducked away in plenty of time. "Ow!" he shouted. Then he whispered to Harry, "That's two!"

Now the kid thought they were both conked out. It was a perfect time to strike. He'd be completely off his guard, trapped on the second floor. "Let's go," Harry said.

Taking the stairs two at a time, both of them raced up to ambush Kevin.

Chapter 21

Above them, Kevin waited patiently. When he heard the footsteps coming up — *really* coming up — he lifted the metal pipe off the floor. One end of the rope was tied firmly around the middle of the pipe. The other end was tied to the railing.

Holding the pipe over his head, he walked to the top of the stairs and let fly.

Harry and Marv looked like two deer caught in a car's headlights. They froze, their eyes bugged open.

"Aaaaaaaaah!" they screamed in unison.

The pipe clipped them both across the

chest. It lifted them off their feet and sent them downward to the foyer . . .

And through the foyer floor into the basement.

They hit the cement with a crunch. Marv slowly raised himself up on his elbows. "That's three," he said.

On the second floor, Kevin took out his jackknife. The pipe was swinging over the stairwell on the rope. He leaned down and cut the pipe loose. It fell to the stairs and began rolling down.

Harry and Marv looked up. They were just in time to see the pipe roll over the edge of the foyer floor — and give them a final conk on the head.

"That's four," Marv said.

Kevin ran to the end of the second-floor hallway. There, behind the door with the missing knob, was the stairway going up. He pulled open the door and picked up the rope that dangled down from the third floor.

Making a quick loop in the end of the rope, he listened for Harry and Marv. He heard them climbing up from the basement into the foyer. "Do you guys give up?" he called out.

Downstairs, the two men were fuming. At the sound of Kevin's voice, they sprinted up to the second floor, shielding their faces.

"You better say every prayer you ever heard, kid!" Harry shouted.

"I hope your parents got you a tombstone for Christmas!" Marv said.

Kevin stuffed the loop out through the hole. Then he ran up the stairs to the third floor, pulling the door shut behind him.

At the top, he checked the rope he had tied to the handle of the huge tool chest to make sure it was tight. Then he pushed the chest to the very edge of the top step. "I'm up here and I'm really scared!" he said.

Harry and Marv clambered down the second-floor hallway. They stopped when they got to the door. Harry pulled on the loop of rope, expecting the door to swing open.

Instead, three feet of rope came out of the hole. Harry looked at it, baffled.

From behind the door, there was a rhythmic clanking. "What's that sound?" Harry said.

He and Marv put their ears to the door.

WHHHAAAAMMMMM!

The tool chest came slamming into the door. It blew the hinges off the jamb. Harry and Marv flew across the hall and crashed against the opposite wall.

"I think," Marv said as they sank to the floor, "that was the sound of a tool chest falling down the stairs."

Above them, Kevin was scrambling up the stairs and onto the roof. He ran to the edge and tugged at the rope around the bag of cement. It held fast.

The rest of the rope was still coiled in the bucket of kerosene. The leather work gloves were lying faceup on the floor. He put on the gloves, then pulled the rope out of the bucket and draped it over the edge of the roof.

Now everything was set for the final phase.

Harry and Marv made their way to the third floor, then hobbled up toward the roof. "I don't care if I get the electric chair," Harry muttered. "I'm *killing* that kid!"

"If we can catch him," Marv said.

"We'll catch him," Harry shot back. "He's on the roof. Where's he going to go?"

"Last time he went to a tree house."

Kevin heard their voices. He stepped over the side of the roof, holding tightly onto the kerosene-soaked rope. Then he slid down. The kerosene made the rope slippery, but the leather gloves gave him a decent grip. He landed on the scaffold, let go of the rope, and whipped off the gloves.

Above him, Harry kicked open the roof door. "Surrender, kid!" he yelled.

Marv peered around. "I don't see him, Harry."

"I'm down here, you morons!" Kevin shouted.

Harry and Marv ran to the side of the roof and looked over.

Kevin was standing on the scaffold, next to the open cans of varnish. He waved cheerfully to them. "Nice night for a neck injury."

"Let's get him," Marv murmured to Harry. He grabbed the rope.

Harry slapped him across the face. "Are you nuts?"

"What?"

"That's exactly what he wants us to do! Have you got a memory?"

Harry took the rope from Marv. He gave it a tug. It seemed secure. Just to make sure, he checked to see where it was tied.

He spotted the bag of cement. His lips curled into a crafty smile.

"What?" Marv asked.

"He's smart," Harry said, "but not smart enough."

He went to the cement bag and untied the rope. "A hundred pounds of cement," he said, reading the label. "It'll hold the kid, but it ain't going to hold us. We get on the rope, and down we go. So . . ." Harry quickly tied the rope to a strong, stationary iron pipe. ". . . we'll just have to disappoint the little creep."

"Harry?" Marv said, looking at his partner with admiration. "You're a genius."

Harry went over first, and Marv followed. Neither of them heard Kevin striking a kitchen match on the stack of bricks below them. With a grin, Kevin held the lit match near the end of the rope. The moment it touched the kerosene, flames would shoot straight up toward Harry and Marv.

Marv was not even halfway down when he smelled something funny. "You wearing after-shave?" he called down to Harry.

"What're you talking about?" Harry snapped.

"I smell something."

Harry noticed the rope was wet. He sniffed it. "That ain't after-shave," he said. "It's kerosene. The rope's soaked in it."

"Why would somebody soak a rope in kerosene?" Marv asked.

Harry couldn't figure out the answer to that. Curious, he looked down toward the scaffold.

He saw Kevin's smiling face. Then he saw the flickering match.

Now he knew.

"Merry Christmas," Kevin chimed.

He moved the match to the tip of the rope.

With a flash, the rope ignited. Fire began crackling upward. Kevin stuffed the matchbox in his pack, leapt off the scaffold, and ran down the street.

Harry's eyes bulged with terror. *"Go up!"* he shouted.

He and Marv tried to scramble up the

rope. They groped with their hands, pushed with their feet. The rope jerked wildly.

In a moment, Harry and Marv had their bodies wrapped around a torch. "Aaaaaaaaaaah!"

Their screams rang up and down the street as they let go and fell downward.

Both of them landed smack on the scaffold. It lurched downward. Harry and Marv fell off. The open cans of varnish catapulted into the air.

The two men landed on their backs in the rubble-strewn garden. High above them, the cans tumbled in the air. Varnish spewed out, forming a thick, liquid arc across the moonlit sky.

Harry and Marv could do nothing but stare helplessly as the goo plummeted straight down.

With a loud splash, it coated them from head to toe.

Down the street, at the corner of Central Park West, Kevin grabbed a pay phone and punched 911. He panted breathlessly, his chest heaving. His eyes darted around nervously as he waited. Across the street, pigeons roosted in the trees of Central Park. Over his shoulder, Harry and Marv were picking themselves up in the garden.

Come on, answer! Kevin thought. In his mind, he raced through the final stage of his plan. If it didn't work, this would be his last Christmas on earth.

"Hello?" came a voice on the other end.

Kevin practically shouted into the mouthpiece. "Hello! The two guys who robbed Duncan's Toy Chest are in the park, at Central Park West and Ninety-sixth Street! You'll see a bright light! Hurry! They've got a gun!"

He slammed the receiver down and looked up the street. Harry and Marv were now climbing over the garden railing. Harry was reaching for his gym bag. "I'm down here!" Kevin shouted. "Come and get me before I call the cops!"

The two men immediately began limping up the street. Their faces were twisted with agony as they forced their battered bodies forward.

Kevin turned to cross the street, but he stopped short. A bus was crossing the intersection, slowing down to let off passengers at the next block.

The delay was costly. Harry and Marv were gaining ground. Kevin could smell the varnish.

Racing around the back of the bus, he crossed Central Park West. He leapt onto the curb on the opposite side.

His feet came down on a patch of ice. They slipped forward, pitching Kevin into the air. He came down hard on the sidewalk, skidding into the park wall. The strap of his backpack broke and the pack flew off.

Kevin sat up, dazed. He could see Harry and Marv across the street now. Marv spotted him and pointed.

Scrambling to his feet, Kevin ran to the backpack and scooped it off the ground. He cast a panicked look back across the street.

Another bus went by, blocking his view. When it passed, the opposite side of Central Park West was empty. Harry and Marv were gone.

Confused, Kevin stared for a split second. Then he turned and ran.

He got only a few steps when he felt a hand grip his shoulder. With a gasp, he looked up into Harry's sooty, bruised face.

In a voice that froze the blood in Kevin's veins, Harry said, "Let's go for a stroll."

He pulled Kevin through the entrance into Central Park. Then he grabbed Kevin's backpack and slammed him into a rock formation.

Ripping the pack open, he dug out the Polaroids. Marv looked over his shoulder.

He held one photo up into the light of the street lamp. There they were in Duncan's Toy Chest, looking stupid, their hands full of cash.

Harry chuckled. "This'll look nice in the photo album."

"Hey, look," Marv said, pulling out Kevin's Talkboy.

Harry grabbed it, rewound the tape a little, then pressed PLAY.

"*. . . we ain't robbing houses no more,*" came Marv's voice. "*We're robbing toy stores. Tonight, we're hitting Duncan's Toy Chest. . . .*"

Harry clicked it off.

"Hey, that was me," Marv said with a smile.

"The little jerk was taping us," Harry said, pulling out the cassette. He threw Kevin's pack to the ground and stuffed the cassette and the photos into his gym bag.

"You may have won the battle, little dude," Marv said, "but you lost the war."

Harry smirked. "You oughtn't not mess around with us, pal. We can be dangerous."

Suddenly Harry's smirk disappeared. His clammy, varnish-smeared hand lurched forward.

Kevin tried to back off, but Harry grabbed him by the neck. "Should we burn his hair off?" Harry snarled.

"How about we *rip* it off?" Marv suggested.

"Throw him in a basement?" Harry said, his voice dripping with mockery.

"Bomb him with a sewer pipe?"

With each word, Harry's grip tightened. Kevin couldn't breathe. He clutched at Harry's hand, but the man was too strong.

"I have a better idea," Harry said. With his free hand, he reached into the gym bag.

Kevin stiffened with fear as Harry slowly pulled out a gun.

Chapter 22

Visions of his mother and father raced through Kevin's mind. He knew they would be mad at him for getting lost at the airport. He knew they'd probably yell, and Buzz would make his life miserable.

But he would give anything — *anything* to be with them again.

Harry raised the gun toward Kevin. Kevin shook. It didn't look like his wish was going to be granted.

Behind Harry and Marv, a figure appeared in the shadows. It moved slowly toward them. Kevin caught it in the corner of his eye.

Pigeons began flocking by the dozens

into the tree branches. They came from all directions, their wings fluttering loudly.

Marv looked up. "Harry?" he said.

"Shut up!" Harry barked.

The figure moved closer, unseen by the two men.

Marv was getting nervous. The birds bothered him. The birds and . . . something else. He couldn't figure out what. "Let's get out of here," he said. "Something's wrong."

"I said shut up!" Harry glared at Kevin, his eyes like lasers. "I didn't get past the sixth grade. Looks like you won't, either."

Click. Harry cocked the gun. Kevin closed his eyes and swallowed hard.

"Let him go."

The voice was soft and creaky — but it cut through the silence like a shout. Harry and Marv spun around.

The figure stepped out of the shadows. Her clothes were rags, her face craggy and covered with filth, but her eyes burned with fierce determination.

In her right hand she held a bucket. Before Harry or Marv could say a word, she threw it toward them.

They cringed in surprise. Harry released Kevin.

Birdseed pelted the two men like a thick hailstorm. It stuck to the varnish, coating them from head to toe. Reeling backward, they coughed and spat.

Kevin looked upward. In unison, the pigeons spread their wings.

Feeding time!

They swooped downward, filling the sky, blocking the streetlight. Harry and Marv peered through the sticky seed on their faces. They gasped in horror.

The birds converged on them, covering both men in a blanket of feathers, beaks, and claws. Harry and Marv fell to the ground, flailing helplessly.

In the distance, Kevin heard the faint screaming of police sirens. He scooped up his backpack and took out the flare and matches. Then he raced out to the park entrance and set up the flare in the road.

That would tip off the police, just as he had planned. He wished he could stay there, but it was too risky. After all, he was a fugitive, too.

As the sirens got louder, Kevin scampered back into the park. He ran behind a boulder and hid. Maybe he couldn't show his face, but at least he could have the satisfaction of watching.

In all the rush and confusion, Kevin didn't notice the pigeon lady shuffling back into the shadows.

With a screech of brakes, two squad cars raced into the park. They fishtailed to a stop right beside the flare.

Kevin peered through a crack in the rock. He saw four cops jumping out of the cars. He watched them pull out their guns and walk toward the boulder. And he watched an identical look of amazement come over their faces.

Harry and Marv were on their feet now. Their arms and legs jerked about in a desperate dance as they tried to shake off the birds. But the pigeons clung to them, ignoring their screams, pecking furiously at the seed.

Dumbfounded, the cops just stared. No one seemed to know how to handle this.

Finally one of them took out his revolver and pointed it to the sky.

POW!

The shot resounded, echoing off the nearby buildings. In a frightened flurry, the pigeons flew away. They disappeared quickly into the distance like a receding rain cloud.

Harry and Marv turned to face the police. Kevin could hardly recognize them. Gray and white feathers stuck to their full-body coat of varnish, making them look like a bizarre species of giant bird. Among the feathers were clots of birdseed and big white splotches of pigeon poop.

Meekly they put their hands over their heads. A few gray and white feathers floated gently to the ground.

One of the policemen picked up Harry's gym bag and unzipped it. He looked inside at the money, the cassette, and the photos.

"I guess these are the guys," he said, looking at the photos. "Arrest them."

Two of the other cops approached Harry and Marv with handcuffs. "All right, fellas," one of them said. "On the ground, hands behind you."

The two crooks obeyed without a word. As one cop cuffed them, the other recited their rights. "You have the right to remain silent, anything you say can be used against you in a court of law, you have a right to retain a lawyer . . ."

Behind the boulder, Kevin was ecstatic. "This is *great!*" he whispered.

Operation Ho Ho Ho was a success. Harry and Marv were heading back to jail. The cops had the money, and they knew where it came from. Mr. Duncan would be making his trip to the Children's Hospital tomorrow. Kevin had done his good deed.

Considering he was on the lam in a strange city in the wee hours of Christmas morning, Kevin felt pretty good.

It was time to move on. The last thing he needed was to be thrown in jail with the birdmen. He ducked behind the rock and slipped away into the night.

Hiding behind the gnarled trunk of a tree, the pigeon lady watched him. Her eyes followed his movement until he was swallowed up by the shadows.

Casting her sad eyes downward, she walked away.

Chapter 23

Harry and Marv left a trail of feathers and seed as they were escorted to the squad car.

Harry was blind with anger. His money, his new life, his freedom — it was all gone. And because of that snotty kid!

No. It wasn't the kid. He and Marv had escaped the boobytrap. They had outfoxed the little creep.

If it weren't for that . . . for that . . .

Could it have been? This was like a fairy tale — some ragtag fairy godmother waltzes in out of nowhere and saves the kid's miserable life. And now he and Marv were going to prison. For the rest of their lives they'd be talking to halfwits, eating terrible food, sleeping on scratchy mattresses, all because of . . .

Birdseed.

For the first time in his life, Harry wanted to cry.

"You guys should have started a little earlier," cracked one of the officers. "The prisoners already exchanged gifts."

"Well," Marv explained, "we had to hide out until the — "

Harry kneed him. "Why don't you shut up, Marv? Didn't the guy just say we got the right to remain silent?"

The officer shoved Harry into the backseat.

"He's a little cranky," Marv said. "You see, we just broke out of jail a few days ago — "

The officer pushed Marv in, too. He slammed the door, leaving the two crooks in their piles of goop. As the officer drove to the precinct house, he looked back through the rearview mirror and watched Harry and Marv all the way.

He wondered how on earth he'd ever get the backseat clean again.

* * *

Asleep in a plush, comfortable armchair, Peter McCallister snored softly. His wife sat by the hotel room window. It was the first time she'd sat since they got to the Plaza. Outside, bells tinkled and Christmas lights blinked gaily, but she noticed none of it. Somewhere out there, in that vast city, her son was wandering lost.

That is, if he wasn't . . .

She grabbed a magazine. She needed *something* to distract the awful thoughts that were tumbling around in her head.

Absentmindedly she flipped through the pages. There were mostly articles about New York: an interview with a local newswoman, restaurant advice, play reviews, a picture of the tree at Rockefeller Center . . .

She flipped a couple more pages, then stopped. Quickly she turned back to the tree.

"World's Largest Christmas Tree," the caption said. It was stunning, decorated with thousands of tiny lights and a giant star on top.

She stared and stared at it. She realized it was the one thing that had caught her attention. That must mean *something*, she thought.

She just wasn't sure what.

Chapter 24

BING-BING-BING-BONNNNNG!

Kevin looked up. The spires of a cathedral rose above Fifth Avenue. In between strokes of the bell, Kevin could hear a choir through the church's open door.

It was beautiful. *They really know how to sing in New York*, Kevin thought.

There were hundreds of people inside. Lots of them were kids, staying up late for Christmas mass. Kevin wondered if there were any kids in the choir. Maybe one of them was holding electric candles behind another one's ears.

He laughed. Then he felt tears welling up in his eyes.

Kevin lowered his head and kept walking. He kicked a paper cup on the sidewalk, swerved around pretzel salesmen. A horse-and-buggy driver called out, "Have a Christmas ride with your family?"

He swerved away, right into the path of a man holding a book of photographs. "Pictures with the tree!" he called out. "Souvenirs of a lifetime!"

Kevin looked at the man's photos. Each one showed some family standing in front of a humongous Christmas tree. He knew about that tree. It was the one at Rockefeller Center, in New York City—

Kevin's eyes rose from the photo book. There was a long pathway in front of him. Down the center of it, white statues of angels faced away from him, blowing slender trumpets skyward.

He looked up, following the direction of the trumpets. The sadness in his face melted.

There, at the end of the pathway, was the tree. The one and only, hugest, most beautiful Christmas tree in the world.

He walked closer. Around him, a few

people were straggling away, arm in arm. The skating rink below was smooth and empty. To his left, a man in an official-looking brown overcoat swept the walk.

Kevin stood before the tree, looking up. Its lights shone down at him. The night's chill was loosening its grip. Slowly he felt himself warm to a spirit he hadn't thought he could feel anymore.

In that moment, so much became clear to him. The crazy day, the accident at the airport — the whole trip began to make some sort of sense.

He spoke in a soft voice to the tree. "I know I don't deserve a Christmas, even if I did do a good deed. I don't want any presents. Instead I want to take back every mean thing I ever said to my family — even if they don't take back the things they said. I don't care."

He began speaking louder. He had nothing to be ashamed of now, nothing to lose. His backpack, his gadgets, his ticket — all gone. He couldn't even use his name now without risking trouble. All he had left was the truth in his heart. A truth he was just discovering. "I love all of them," he said. "Including Buzz. But

. . . if it isn't possible for me to see all of them, could I just see my mother? I'll never want another thing as long as I live. I just want my mother. I know I won't see her tonight, but promise me I can see her again. Sometime. Anytime. Even if it's just once, for only a couple of minutes. I need to tell her I'm sorry."

There. He said it. It felt good to let it out.

Kevin sighed. The wind was picking up now, and he was starting to feel chilly again. He lowered his head and turned to leave.

Behind him came a faint jingling sound. He stopped. He'd heard that sound before. Funny, it sounded a little like . . .

Ding-a-ling-a-ling!

Like the McCallister family Christmas bell.

Kevin turned around. The talking to the tree must have done something to him. Now he was having visions.

At the end of the block was an apparition of his mother. She was smiling from ear to ear, and Kevin felt a tug of happiness.

The apparition rang the bell again. Kevin walked closer.

Ghosts were supposed to be clear. Well, not *clear*, but you could see through them. At least that was what Kevin thought.

But this was a solid one, just like a real person. And tears were rolling down its cheeks.

"Mom?" Kevin said, his voice tiny and parched.

"Merry Christmas, sweetheart," she answered.

Kevin's mouth dropped open. This was no ghost. "Wow!" he said. "That worked fast!"

She knelt down, reaching toward him.

His feet left the ground. He ran to her, full speed. She folded him tightly in her arms.

Kevin closed his eyes, feeling the embrace he'd never forgotten. He let the last two days blow away like a feather on an icy wind.

"How did you know I was here?" he asked.

"I know you and Christmas trees," she said. "This is the biggest one around. I had a hunch."

She kissed him and stood up. "Let's go and let Dad know you're all right."

"Where's everybody else?"

"They're at the hotel."

"They're in *New York*?"

Kevin's mom shrugged. "They didn't like the palm trees either. Come on."

She put her arm around his shoulder as they headed toward Fifth Avenue. Kevin took one look over his shoulder and saw a thousand lights winking at him.

He winked back.

Chapter 25

E. F. Duncan watched grimly as the police sifted through the mess in his store. He and his wife had come straight from their Christmas party. Under his cashmere overcoat he wore his finest suit. Mrs. Duncan's glittering gown was all but covered by her mink coat.

This was not the way they'd expected to celebrate the holiday.

Ian Josephs, a police evidence specialist, knelt down in the shattered glass of the front window. He picked up a large paving stone and removed the envelope that was banded around it.

As he read the message, a police sergeant strode up to Mr. Duncan. He held a walkie-talkie in his right hand, and he was smiling brightly.

"It's all over, Mr. Duncan," he said. "Our men apprehended the thieves and recovered your money."

The sadness lifted from the Duncans' faces. They hugged each other with joy and relief. "I thank you very much, Sergeant," Mr. Duncan said.

Officer Josephs interrupted them. He held Kevin's note in his hand. "Excuse me. Are you Mr. Duncan?"

"Yes," Mr. Duncan replied.

Handing him the envelope, Officer Josephs said, "This was wrapped around a paver we found over there. Looks like a kid broke your window."

Mr. Duncan lifted the letter from the Plaza envelope and read it:

Dear Mr. Duncan,
   I broke your window to catch the bad guys. I'm sorry. Do you have insurance? If you don't, I'll send you

some money when it snows more (if I ever get back to Chicago).

> *Merry Christmas,*
> *Kevin McCallister*

Mr. Duncan chuckled. He knew who this was. "Turtledoves," he said under his breath.

As the sun peeked over the New York City skyline, the Plaza Hotel staff was already hard at work. Chefs were preparing Christmas breakfasts and checking supplies for dinner. Extra cleaning people were on hand for the celebrations. Waiters eagerly set tables, hoping for extra tip money to take home to their families.

And in the front of the building, delivery men guided a truck marked DUNCAN'S TOY CHEST up to the sidewalk.

When the truck stopped, the delivery men pulled open the rear door. The truck was jammed with presents, wrapped in the finest Christmas paper.

The men loaded the gifts one by one onto hand carts. As they wheeled them into the lobby, they were met by the concierge. "This way," he said.

He led them to the elevator. There, the bellman and the clerk were holding an enormous, fully decorated Christmas tree.

Quietly, with smiles on their faces, they took it all to the fourth floor.

Chapter 26

"Holy smokes! It's morning!"

This year, Fuller was the first McCallister to wake up on Christmas morning.

Kevin and Brooke were sharing the room with him, so they woke up, too.

"It's Christmas morning, man!" Fuller shouted.

Kevin sat up. His eyes were half-shut, his mouth felt cottony. Yes, it was Christmas morning, but all he wanted to do was sleep.

"Fuller?" he said. "Don't get your hopes up."

Fuller looked at him blankly. "Huh?"

"I'm not sure Santa Claus goes to hotels."

"Are you nuts?" Fuller said. "He's omnipresent. He goes everywhere."

He leapt out of bed, screaming, "Wake up! It's Christmas!"

Brooke followed him into the adjoining bedroom. "Wake up, Dad!"

Frank and Leslie McCallister began to stir. Rod and Tracey popped out of their cots.

Fuller and Brooke charged into the living room. They meant to go across it, to the bedroom on the other side.

But they never got there.

When they saw the Christmas tree, loaded with presents, they stopped running. They stared at it, unable to move.

Mr. and Mrs. McCallister came out of the opposite bedroom, stretching. Buzz, Jeff, Linnie, and Megan followed behind them. They took a step into the living room and gaped.

"Are we in the right room?" Buzz asked.

Next came Uncle Frank and Aunt Leslie, with Rod, Tracey, Sondra, and Kevin. Uncle Frank was yawning, big-time.

He was the last to see it. He froze in mid-yawn.

Kevin walked through the room of human statues. His face lit up. He took in the mountain of gifts; the wrapping paper he recognized from Duncan's Toy Chest. "Wow!" was all he could say.

"Whose is whose?" Fuller asked.

"Just pass them around!" Kevin replied.

Fuller and Brooke began picking up gifts and distributing them. Everyone began talking at once.

"Get the camera!" Uncle Frank shouted.

"Careful with the wrapping paper," Aunt Leslie warned. "We can reuse it!"

Suddenly Buzz's voice boomed above them all. "Everybody calm down!"

Fuller and Brooke stopped. The whole family looked at Buzz.

"If Kevin hadn't screwed things up so bad again, we wouldn't be in this most perfect and huge hotel room with a truckload of free stuff." He smiled at his younger brother. "So, it's only fair that he gets to open the first present. Then I'll go, and the rest of you, and so on."

He picked up a present and tossed it to Kevin. "Merry Christmas, Kev."

The entire family burst into applause. Kevin caught the present and bowed. He couldn't believe what he had just heard — but he sure liked it.

Just as he went to open his present, something caught his attention. Something about the tree.

He looked at it carefully. From top to bottom, it was decorated with the objects from the Twelve Days of Christmas.

His eyes went straight to the two turtledoves.

This Christmas was still not complete, he realized. There was one very important thing he needed to do. One last thing before he left New York.

He would do it this morning, as soon as he could break away.

Smiling to himself, he began ripping his present open.

The other thirteen McCallisters were still playing with their toys and games when Kevin sneaked outside. They wouldn't notice him for at least a half hour or so.

But by that time, he'd be back anyway. He wasn't going to have to go far. He could tell that the moment he looked into Central Park. The moment he saw a huge cluster of pigeons in one of the trees.

He crossed the street and hopped the wall into the park. Under the tree was the pigeon lady, tossing seeds to her birds.

"Merry Christmas," Kevin said.

The pigeon lady turned with a start. When she saw Kevin, she waved. "Merry Christmas, Kevin."

The pigeons cleared a path for Kevin as he walked toward her. Gently he reached out and took the seed bucket from her. He set it on the ground, then took her hand.

Opening her fingers, he set a turtledove into her palm.

She looked at him, her brow wrinkled with confusion.

Kevin held up *his* turtledove. "I have one. You have one. As long as we each have a turtledove, we're friends forever."

The pigeon lady smiled. Kevin thought he could see a tear forming in one of her eyes. "Thank you," she said.

Kevin put his turtledove back into his

pocket. It was time to go, before his mom and dad panicked again.

He threw his arms around the pigeon lady. She returned his embrace.

"I won't forget you," Kevin said as they released each other. "Trust me."

A sudden commotion made them both turn around. The entire flock of pigeons was soaring into the sky. They spiraled upward, dipping and gliding high over the city.

Below them, no one seemed to notice. No one except Kevin and his new friend. In their own ways, they were soaring, too.